THE FLIGHT

By AGNIVA GHOSAL

CHAPTER 1

It was a cold afternoon; in mid January, amidst the mist and fog and no sunshine, the plane landed at one of the busiest airport in the world; London Heathrow and the journey began for a young mother with a small child. Zoya; at last managed to overcome the immigration hurdles and arrived at the lounge, she found Shan waiting impatiently. Raza hesitated to go to Shan; having not seen him much before. As they came out and sat in the waiting car; it took off, Zoya found a thick black smoke covering the city. The sun appeared like a disc without any rays. In this semi-daylight everything seemed moving ceaselessly. A thousand noises rising amidst this unending damp and dark labyrinth; the footsteps of a busy crowd, the crunching wheels of cars, the shriek of police cars and ambulances; she felt breathless and lost, clinging to her son, she tried to found solace and hoped if she can return back home immediately; to the peaceful abode of her village; thousands of miles away; awakening from sleep with the magpie perched under the parasol-like huge leaf of the old fig tree and mounds of leaves of Black plum – banyan – jackfruit – oak – pipal lying still everywhere waiting to be blessed by the morning sun.

Zoya has never before stepped out of her village alone and knew nothing outside her little known world, she had seen the sun coming up and going behind the palm trees surrounding the lakeside. But on the day of her marriage; she travelled to the next village with her groom but never had the opportunity to gaze being continuously looked at by the man.

She returned the next day and remained with her family as there was some argument over the age of her groom that erupted immediately after her marriage. Seven months later Raza was born; though her pregnancy was without complexity, giving birth was a very difficult experience and she almost lost her son if there had not been the timely intervention of the doctor; the local Magistrate's wife who was by chance visiting the village during the children's school holidays.

It was in her fate that Zoya managed to beat all odds and gave birth to her son, a rape victim; she and her friend were raped nine months before and her friend murdered; the crime was the product of a conspiracy amongst the local landlord and members of the frontline extremist political outfit getting prominence in the area.

Zoya and her friend were targeted following a mistaken identity, assuming that they are the girls of the local Hindu family still living and occupying land at the centre of the village; to scare the family to sell off their land and belongings and leave for good at the time just before the elections; when the state of Bangladesh, was deeply split by religious divisions and has been prone to mob violence, committed distinctively by members of the dominant religious group with political affiliations against the minorities. Making matters worse, two police officers were also involved in the crime. Zoya's uncles' decided to keep quiet for fear of being ostracized by their wider family and villagers, instead accepted the monetary compensation and decided to get Zoya married outside the village.

Her husband Shan came to get married at the village after spending more than fourteen years in England and luckily Zoya was his pick. It was an arranged marriage and Zoya hardly saw, feel or had any understanding of what was happening to her, before it was all over and she was back to her usual place. The place she knew so well since as a little girl, each and everyone in the village, the roads, the smell of the first rain, the green velvet over the lake and ponds, the wild flowers and the buzzing insects, the foxes living on the edge and the few brick houses most of them in need of urgent repair being eaten up by the salt in the soil exposing wet red bricks during the rainy reason making them look like wounded and bleeding. The mud houses are rebuilt each year after the rains and folks made homeless constantly on the move for a better life somewhere else; Zoya had no knowledge.

Raza was loved by everyone in the house and all his moves cherished; as he gave up bed and started crawling and then taking small steps and ultimately got the balance and decided to run. The grandmother, the matriarch was first responsible for keeping vigil on the child as he slept most of the day but soon it became impossible for her to keep check on the baby, the family; started blaming the paternal genes for any wrong signal that came from him.

Zoya was happy and content with no worries, she was a little girl and spent her days merrily. When Raza was 4 years old, the Postman delivered a letter that came in Zoya's name from England. As she opened the letter, it was from Shan; expressing his desire to call her to England. After many deliberations by her uncles and great-uncles it was decided in favour of

Shan that Zoya and Raza will make the journey and start a new life in the UK.

Slowly started and developed the phone conversations between 22 year old Zoya and her 44 year old husband, a British citizen. Shan was happy and excited to know about Raza. He also contacted a legal firm in the UK to get a check list and started arranging the relevant documentation to be submitted at the British High Commission to sponsor his wife and child. As the application form was completed, Shan was advised to discuss all aspects of his immigration history with his wife by his legal adviser.

Shan never had a chance to discuss anything with his young wife at the time of marriage as he felt that was irrelevant and his only identity revealed- being a British citizen.

CHAPTER 2

Shan, a Bihari, as self identified in immigration perspective; informed the authorities in the UK, linking his ancestry; tracing back to Muslim communities living in pre-Independence Bihar, India, he having first arrived in the UK in mid-1991 from Bangladesh previously leaving the unbearable conditions in the camp in Dhaka, primarily due to the serious abuse and intimidation at the hands of Bangladeshi local authorities and camp volunteers, he was eventually abducted and sold and worked as a bonded labour; in the northern province of Sylhet from the age of 14.

He had to flee the country; again being targeted by the authorities and ultimately arrived into the UK, as a Bihari refugee and applied for asylum. Shan maintained that he had no fixed address in Bangladesh; he had no knowledge about his place of birth or that of his parents; as he had no contact with his parents after being abducted. Shan had remained in the UK; since his initial arrival.

Though Shan's story may seem inherently unlikely but that does not meant that it is untrue

– it was a fact that non Bengali speaking Muslims who migrated to Bangladesh during the partition of the Indian subcontinent had a very bitter experience when West and East Pakistan parted; giving rise to a section of the "choosing to speak an alternative language group" considered as enemies of the newly born state, and for the proponents of the new state they were entirely not in the wrong side to do so; given the atrocities committed on them and that particular group choosing to side with the perpetrators; made them enemies; after the remission of hostilities. Consequently; like others; hidden in the back corners of the world; scattered populations of millions of nobodies, citizens of nowhere, forgotten and neglected by governments, ignored by census takers; Biharis' are left stranded in refugee camps; in Dhaka waiting for repatriation to Pakistan; their 'dream home' that didn't happen. With the passage of time; the stateless Biharis' became amongst the poorest; and the most disenfranchised. Without citizenship, they could not sent their children to school, had no access to health care or property ownership. Nor they could vote or travel freely outside their cramped camps; particularly young boys and girls were preyed upon by the underworld and sold within Bangladesh or trafficked to India.

The Biharis' became stateless for many reasons; starting from their decision to migrate to East Pakistan as refugees and failure to assimilate with the ethnic population, eventually resulted in them being subjected to ethnic exclusion, instigated by the quirks of history. However; they remained the most vulnerable segment of the population in Bangladesh; after the partition of Pakistan until they were eventually granted citizenship by Bangladesh; more recently. Till that time; Biharis' in Bangladesh; living in the refugee camps had few avenues for redressing abuses, and little access to resources that could help them build better lives and they had few advocates. Therefore; Shan's postal application for asylum identifying himself as "a stateless person" meant that his claim was a valid one under the purview of the Convention.

When Shan arrived in the UK and made his application; according to western calculations; there were estimated hundreds of thousands of Biharis in 66 different camps throughout Bangladesh; and they were stamped "stateless" by the West.

Shan, declared himself to the Home Office as 'a Bihari' in 1992, after much window shopping and expert advice; his sole motive was to get settled in the heaven, obviously he came from a place that lacked everything.

Shan had never been to school, even the basic Bengali script was like Latin to him; being an illiterate eventually proved to be of enormous help. However; he had two exceptional qualities; extremely hardworking and always had the ability to judge what was best for him.

CHAPTER 3

Shan had actually come into the UK; in 1991, using a Bangladeshi passport by road via France with the help of an agent in Bangladesh. He grew up in a farming family, living in a mud-wrapped house with his parents and two siblings, on the banks of river Jamuna. Every year, after the rains; Jamuna burst banks bringing absolute misery to the settlements. Shan's family had to shift to the camp; situated on a high ground, at the village High School. Returning only to discover, the collapsed mud walls and everything washed away.

Having seen extreme poverty from such close, Shan had always worked alongside his father in the field and looked after the cattle. Life was a struggle. His only encounter with school was during the floods each year. Born ten years before the liberation war, his father had on many occasions helped the fighters acting as an informer. Shan had heard innumerable stories of heroism of the freedom fighters from his father that unknowingly shaped his life, in absence of any formal education, to take up new challenges. Immediately upon his arrival Shan was catered by a friend from the same village; Hamid who had arrived few years before taking up the challenge to leave the misery and poverty in the country; to have a better life. Hamid took great care of Shan initially and took him to Shalu Miah, owner of a recruitment agency in Brick Lane, East London.

The registration fee of 10 pounds was also paid by Hamid, Shalu Miah asked Shan to return the next day. Within days Shan was directed to a sleeping picturesque coastal village in south west England; Helston in Cornwall to work at a Bangladeshi Restaurant run by two brothers; Ali & Rois.

Ali; a typical businessman was extremely hardworking and soft spoken to staff; he still struggled to speak English but had a competitive spirit and excellent culinary skills that made his restaurant the most popular amongst the local English populace who lined up on weekends to enjoy a meal and the popularity shot up with time; long after Ali stopped being the Chef and became the Manager; managing everything singlehanded.

His younger brother; Rois was a stylish man who was totally disassociated from the restaurant and had aspirations of becoming a political leader. Despite his non contribution, he received the profit from the business in equal share and represented the restaurant every year at the London Curry Awards and siphoned off the first prize or as a runner up.

Despite being a boaster, Rois was subservient to his elder brother; Ali who spent his entire time running the curry restaurant successfully. His impulsive and speculative temperament urged him to throw himself unreservedly into many challenges including introducing new dishes with weird names and combinations with a fusion of cream, sugar and spices that had never existed in the culinary list from the Indian subcontinent.

However; his experiments yielded results as the new dishes were relished and liked by his customers; white British who queued up on the weekends after a visit to the Pub or Club to satisfy their palate.

Ali and Rois' father had arrived into the UK from pre-partition India in the thirties sailing from the Port City of Calcutta, embarking on a month-long voyage in the underbelly of a steamship, feeding coal into the hungry furnace, literally stoking the fire of commerce, helping to keep the British trade alive; the source of wealth of the mighty far- fetched British Empire at that time.

Ali and Rois; born and raised in Bangladesh later arrived into the UK; aged 23 and 15 years; having granted Right of Abode in the UK; posing as sons of another old Bangladeshi man, who acquired British nationality before they were born, in lieu of a payment made by their father to Fazlu Miah in the UK and transfer of agricultural land in the name of Fazlu Miah's son in Sylhet.

Therefore Ali & Rois had no ties with Bangladesh; having lost their mother early and their father remarried his third wife (35years junior to him) having five children from the marriage, who arrived into the UK as his dependants in the late seventies. Ali & Rois were non- existent in the family tree of their father, submitted to the UK authorities, having used fraudulent visas to arrive initially with full right, to enjoy all facilities at par with a British citizen and after merely a year the boys were registered as British citizens, in their own right.

Their extreme modest background and severe limitations in all fields did not act as a hindrance, being in a close net community, tremendously helped the boys initially and appropriate legal help; awarded them with the lottery; a red passport, obliterating their past and gave them the opportunity to change everything for the better and they did not let the opportunity go waste. However; their father was not fortunate enough to enjoy his family life in the UK with his young wife and five children; the eldest son being 17 at that time and died of a heart attack in London shortly after their arrival; leaving his wife and five children at the council flat in Pimlico; beside river Thames opposite West-Minister House.

Ali & Rois though had very limited contact with their father at any time; but after his death supported their step mother and step-siblings and exploited their step brother at the best possible way; training him excessively to take up the post of the chef, after Ali.

Extreme poverty in Bangladesh, repeated neglect, disrespect had shaped Ali as a slippery and elusive subject, who managed to come out of all adversaries while running his business, his traditional values and absolute lack of knowledge about labour welfare and laws made him the most ignorant of the successful curry businessman in the UK; who managed to toss around in the turbulent seas of UK economy taking advantage of the most disadvantaged from his homeland who were not so lucky to have successfully managed to dodge the UK authorities from the start and were therefore not legally allowed to work.

Therefore; the quest for a better life in the UK altered the paternity of them; two but having seen poverty from close and being neglected; Ali and Rois knew that hard work is the only way to move forward and they did so, from the day of arrival. With plenty of jobs available in the Asian Restaurant Industry in all parts of the country; the duo moved to Stirling in Scotland and started working for an Indian Restaurant owned by a Pakistani. Ali started as a full-time kitchen porter while Rois was enrolled at a local School and worked at night on weekends. The sole purpose of Ali moving to Scotland was free accommodation and free food. Though the brothers had no access to any social benefits due to their fraudulent status but they had no problem and were without any expenses.

Ali started work with £50 a week wage; working 13hours a day and Rois got £20 for long busy weekends but they never complained. The extreme cold and long winter in Scotland further restricted their movements. They had no friends, no private life, no social life; the place of work was everything to them. Ali also tried the best in his capacity to shield Rois from everything as the undercurrent of the defeat in Bangladesh and the tension between Pakistani's and Bangladeshi's flared up unduly and frequently whenever someone; a protagonist of the Bangladeshi freedom struggle arrived to work at the restaurant in Scotland.

Ali was keen to save all the money; they earned and not having a bank account meant he had to carry it everywhere. He worked in the restaurant for two long years, allowing Rois to finish school. Thereafter the brothers decided to move to the south of the border; having managed to find employment in the picturesque town of Keswick in Cumbria and worked there continuously for 5 years.

Actually after a probationary period of two years in Scotland, it was during these crucial years that Ali and Rois learned the tricks of life in Britain and they became proficient in their chosen fields. Ali became a chef; learning the art of cooking through observation and by applying common sense. He had in the next seven years; seldom set foot outside the restaurant kitchen; spending on an average; 14 hours in the kitchen; observation was the key to his success.

However; Rois was outgoing and while attending college in Keswick; he made some friends locally and developed a social life. He often during the weekdays ventured around the town centre of Keswick; by the beautiful lake side; had a pint of beer at the local pub and visited the Oxfam charity shop to buy used branded cloths; and gradually developed growing dissatisfaction with ordinary clothes and shoes, in fact over time; he became a 'brand slave', seeing Rois, one could easily had a feeling that he had integrated well, putting down roots, but the word integration implies so much more than simply being able to pick up the language and adapting to the mores of a new country; as people are not machines that can be reset and re-programmed to fit the desired cultural make-up, the struggle within him to perpetuate the cultural values from home was constant.

CHAPTER 4

When Ali was 12 and Rois 4, their father married 35 years junior, 20 year old, Luthfunissa Begum; in 1969, in Bangladesh, an event that shattered their lives into pieces. Their mother was mentally unstable, she had married Abdul Latif, a British man who spoke fluent English; in 1956, when he visited East Pakistan after spending 26 years; in the UK and was married to an Irish woman and had children. The marriage was arranged by her brothers. Soon; she was abandoned and had to manage the pregnancy alone. As Latif maintained very little contact with his family in Bangladesh; gradually their mother's mental health deteriorated; she having inherited it from her maternal side. However; Latif returned to Bangladesh after seven years and met his son; Ali the first time. Despite being in a fragile mental health at that time; their mother again became pregnant and gave birth to Rois in 1965.But unfortunately; their mother died at childbirth; it was Ali who had to look after his brother since from a young age and in a real sense; brought him up.

Abdul Latif returned to Bangladesh, the third time in 1969 and married his third wife. He had five children, Aklas, Shirin, Anu, Rima and Rina born in Bangladesh in 1970, 1972 and 1974 and 1977 and 1979. Their step-mother and five step-siblings arrived into the UK, legally in 1985 as the second wife and children of Abdul Latif.

Ali and Rois had always longed for a cosy family home with parents and siblings; an invitation from their father was what they needed to shred off all ties with Cumbria and move to London. The chance came when their father; Abdul Latif was admitted at Guy's Hospital and their step-brother; Aklas called them; as per the wish of their father. Ali and Rois took no time to resign; losing a week's wage for not giving enough notice to their Pakistani employer and reached the bus station; the next morning with all belongings. After a tiring journey of ten hours they reached London; Victoria Bus Station.

Throughout the journey; Rois' grim face gave Ali the feeling that things are not ok for him. However; he couldn't anticipate what was bothering his brother; since they were never emotionally bonded with their father. Though; Aklas was supposed to be at the Bus Station and take them to their flat in Pimlico but he couldn't be found. After waiting patiently for a while; Aklas came rushing and apologised to Ali. They took the underground, and the next station was Pimlico. Ali and Rois for the first time stepped into their family home; they felt awkward and alienated; heard crying of their step-mother from the next room. They hardly had any sleep.

Next morning; the brothers went to Guys Hospital; to see their father after ages. Their father; was suffering from a lung disease-byssinosis, having spent a significant time working in the Mill where the air was filled with thick cotton dust and had a myocardial infarction; last week, he was serious. At 73; there was little strength left in him and the anguish and pain was literally visible in his face. Ali felt bad as their father begged him for mercy and asked for forgiveness. It seemed to Rois that his father has prepared himself to face the inevitable, death. Abdul Latif died the same day. When the nurse came and gave the news that Mr Latif has passed away peacefully; Ali was left in a shock; wandering; the man whom he had hated since childhood the most, who he blames directly responsible for his mother's mental instability and premature death, has left the world, wondering; Where has he gone? Where will he be? Whether he will get the right punishments for his misdeeds? And so on. Standing beside his brother; Rois thought about his father; as a fearless soul; who decided to sail across the ocean to see the unseen and for a better life, a man of mixed qualities who had obviously longed for a long marital life with his third wife and children but it was cut short.

CHAPTER 5

Abdul Latif; their father came into UK, in 1930;during the British Raj from undivided India, aged 16 at that time; working in the ship as a fireman and never went back. England in 1930s was not the best of the places, it was a time when the Government rode roughshod over the already impoverished working class, reducing wages and benefits; plunging the living standards of the working class in the name of National Economic measures while it continued to spend millions of pounds on armaments and preparation for a war that slaughtered millions of workers including those in other countries and all in the interest of capitalism.

Being in his early teens; Abdul Latif easily assimilated to British life, he met; Janet; an Irish woman from Northern Ireland, in 1933, who had fled the Catholic Monastery in London Derry and arrived at Liverpool in search of a better life. They met in a Pub at Scotland Road; close to both the back end of the city centre and the docks; which was a hub of migrant communities but Latif was the only Asian man there.

Though Latif and Janet had nothing in common but both in their twenties; found love and started living together, sharing a small two up and two down terraced house with two other couples. Latif was working in the local Shipyard while Janet was the washer woman in the local laundry. In 1934; their eldest son; Carney was born in the harsh winter months. Janet's aunt Elizabeth who was visiting Liverpool, from Canada named the child 'Carney' from 'cearnach' meaning "victorious".

After Carney was born; Janet had to give up work and loss of employment meant the couple was forced into a state; just above the poverty threshold. But thanks to the Government initiative to build new housing, post World War 1 that helped the couple re-house from the inner-city to a new suburban housing estate based on the pretext that this would improve their standard of living, though this was largely subjective.

Latif had to increase his working hours and couple was really struggling. They just had enough money for food, rent, fuel and clothes. They could not afford 'luxuries' such as newspapers or public transport. Like so many of that generation they only bought what they could pay for. This was the time before plastic bags and things were often sold without packaging in the shops; items would be weighed out and put loose right into shopping bags or maybe, wrapped in brown paper bags or newspaper and were stored in their respective containers at home by Janet.

Biscuits were put into the biscuit barrel and then the paper bag that they came wrapped in was straightened out and folded up and put away ready to be used to wrap something else up in it. Absolutely nothing was wasted. Potatoes in the greengrocers were sold from Hessian sacks that contained 56lbs of potatoes.

Because everything they bought was a necessity nothing was wasted and items were often used more than once. Even when things came tied up with string; Janet would un-tie the string not cut and then wound it up and put away to use again. In the case of the Hessian sacks that the potatoes were stored in at the greengrocers; Janet often collected empty sacks from the greengrocer and then used as a foundation to make a Peg Rug that she sold for a small remuneration.

Jumpers and cardigans required by the family were hand knitted not shop bought and when they got too worn then the garment was unpicked and the wool re-used to knit the new jumper or cardigan. Latif's hard work in the docks meant that when his socks' got holes in them they would be darned as would any woollen garment by Janet using a Darning Mushroom. Another important tool was the Cobbler's Last which was used by Latif to repair his shoes.

Janet also often re-used worn out adult clothing to make children's clothing; and kept the buttons and elastic for re-use. When items could no longer be reused as clothing then she used them for other things such as cleaning rags or cut up to make Peg rugs.

They had a penny in the slot gas meter for the gas which was used for lighting and the gas stove. If they didn't have a penny for the meter then they didn't get any gas and cannot have gas heating in the house. With the temperature inside the house same as outside often plunging to sub zero; ice started forming inside of the windows and the couple had no choice but to wear overcoats inside the house.

When there was not enough money to meet the necessities of life one resource that was commonly used by Janet was the local Pawn Shop. The symbol for a Pawn Brokers was three balls hanging outside the shop and there was an old joke about what the three balls signified "Two to one, you won't get your stuff back". During desperate hours, Janet would often take items of value to the Pawn Brokers and take a loan for a fixed rate of interest with the premise that if she paid back the loan and the interest in the time agreed she could redeem the item. Most of the time this did not happen and the items were later sold off by the Pawn Broker to get his money back. Janet also loved looking in the Pawn Shop windows as there was so much interesting stuff displayed in there; without thinking about the emotions attached to those old valuables.

CHAPTER 6

With the declaration of war to the people; on 3rd September 1939 via the radio; life of the working class changed in Britain for ever. There was rationing, manpower allocation, home defence, evacuation in the face of air raids, in response to preparation against any possibility of occupation of the country by an enemy power.

One of the hardest things many people had to deal with in major cities like London, Liverpool, Birmingham and Portsmouth which were deemed as likely targets for the German Luftwaffe was the evacuation of the children and pregnant women. The evacuation of vulnerable children from the large cities were designed to send the children temporally to what was considered the much safer country side villages and small market towns out of harm's way from the expected bombing; called Operation Pied Piper. There were three waves of evacuation during the war; the first one took place before the declaration of the war; on 1[ST]September 1939.But as nothing bad happened during the initial months and people started calling it "the phoney war"; 60% of the children who were evacuated returned to their homes.

Janet was reluctant to leave Liverpool with Carney despite Latif's insistence to do so. As the war proceeded through the years; Janet and Latif gradually learnt to get used to blackout, rationing and nothing but work to help the country pass through war time believing that the end of the war will create a fairer world.

To avoid aiding German bombers, all lights after dusk were banned. At first; it seemed a novelty and some people walked around looking at the darkness and the starlit night sky. But it quickly became one of the biggest annoyances of wartime life. Both driving and walking in the dark were very difficult and dangerous. Shopping hours were cut and even little things like paying for a bus became a trial in the dark.

Another hardship was rationing, Petrol was on ration from 1939 then from January 1940 essential food items such as butter, sugar, eggs and bacon were put on ration and the list kept on expanding. In March 1940 all meat became rationed, by July; tea and margarine joined the list and still the list was growing. It was very hard for the mothers of young families already living pretty near the poverty line before the war to cope with it. By March 1941; Jam joined the list and in May; so did cheese followed in June;

by the rationing of all textiles and clothing. It seemed like everything useful or necessary was to join this list of rationing, in 1942; soap, coal, gas, electricity, sweets, chocolate and biscuits were also added to this list with sausages being added in the following year. Extreme rationing of all essential items; brought discontent amongst the working class as it affected their dietary habits while people with money could buy almost everything in the black market. People were forced to get introduced to new foods like dried egg and other preserved food items which was previously obtained fresh from the market. The only benefit of rationing was that it helped the working class to have a balanced diet. The government was aware of the impact of rationing on morale and never rationed bread, potatoes, cigarettes or beer. Because; rationing affected everyone; it did create a sense of shared sacrifice during war time that cut across class lines. But eating at restaurants was not rationed; therefore those with money did have access to more food. Also; violent crimes; in cities rose sharply during 1939 to 1945.

Despite the Government propaganda machine being active; people like Janet and Latif were cynical about the outcome of the war that forced them to change everything and was soon forced into separation.

Due to their strategic importance, Liverpool, Birkenhead, Bootle and Wallasey soon became the most heavily bombed areas of the country; outside of London that experienced heavy German bombing and the desperate attempt by the state machinery to hide the news from the enemies about the extent of damage suffered.

The Mersey's docks provided anchorage for naval ships from many nations and handled over 90 per cent of all the war material brought into Britain from abroad; thousands of tons of material were then transferred to small boats and transported to various parts of the country through the extensive network of quays. Liverpool was the eastern end of a transatlantic chain of supplies from North America, without which Britain could not have pursued the war, which obviously made it a prime target by the Germans.

Immediately following Janet's refusal to part from Latif; the couple decided to move house in July 1940; moving to a coastal village; just north of Southport, called Banks, situated on the Ribble estuary. It was a quite village with cheap housing and most residents being involved in agriculture, even those not farmers themselves would help the farmers during the busy times of the year such as during hay-making and harvest. Most people were employed in the local area. Everyone knew everyone else except this young Indo-European family who arrived from nowhere raising eyebrows amongst the older generation; many of whom had never seen an Asian man before and have never heard the word, 'Muslim'.

Many of the older generation were unhappy with the new addition; blaming the damn war; causing change in the villages too. In the village; though daily work and life still continued almost as usual; except the Government machinery; taught the people to become more vigilant, so the sudden arrival of Latif and Janet with a small child was a matter of suspicion and the couple remained under the scanner for some time. Duty at the busy wartime docks in Liverpool meant Latif stayed outside of home during majority of the week and Janet was living alone with Carney but as practically anything could be bought or mended in the village, she faced little difficulties.

To save money and to be close to the work place Latif shared a room with four Irish migrants; all his room-mates were heavy drinkers and always spend the last penny to get drunk. Most of the nights Latif was awaked by an odd shower as the man sleeping above him in the bunk bed had no sense to use the toilet. The men were voracious eaters too and ate almost raw meat just turning in once on the pan; leaving Latif astonished. They all had huge families in Ireland and had come to Liverpool to earn a living.

Latif was in his room when the first major air raid on Liverpool took place in the summer of 1940, everyone run for the shelters except his four drunken room-mates who could not be awaked despite Latif's best efforts and had to be abandoned. Thereafter; bombing raid became a regular event in Liverpool and Latif got used to it like others; sometime bombing lasted for few minutes but it became a matter of great concern when it lasted for days and caused massive destruction, particularly when air raid shelters were directly hit there were massive loss of lives.

Though the severity of air raids decreased in the New Year but again there was a renewal of the air assault since Spring of 1941 when a seven night bombing of the region destroyed the much important docks, ships docked there stacked with ammunition, important buildings and infrastructure and the loss of innocent lives were irreversible.

After the raids in the Spring of 1941, the German air assault diminished, as Hitler's attention turned towards attacking the Soviet Union. The last German air raid on Liverpool took place in the winter of 1942; destroying several houses including the house where Alois Hitler Jr., half brother of Adolf Hitler had once lived. Latif was extremely saddened when St Luke's Church, at the city centre was gutted during the firebombing; given his emotional attachment with it; he and Janet got married there and she was a regular visitor, also Carney was baptised in the same Church.

The forced separation of the couple meant that Janet was left constantly worried about Latif and village life was becoming very difficult for her to settle into. There was constant monitoring by the local residents and very often bizarre spying stories emerged from nowhere. Janet was left baffled when members of the local Home Guard service set up to keep law and order in the villages and provide protection to the inhabitants started visiting her house during black-outs to investigate the inhabitants of the house situated on the hill opposite to her house as light flashes regularly appeared from the house which some had already interpreted as a sort of message; using the Morse code.

The house on the hill was occupied by an elderly couple and their four grand-children who had been evacuated from London. The couple's daughter and son-in-law were also regular visitors and there was rumour in the village that the son-in-law has been dismissed from military service.

As weeks of investigations remained unresolved; the local Police chief accompanied by members of the Home guard at last visited the house and discovered that it was the reflection of the kitchen light by a mirror hanging in the toilet door; situated in the courtyard whenever anyone opened the toilet door at night. It soon became a laughing matter in the village.

Though Janet felt lonely and desolate most of the time but she tried her best to keep herself busy particularly during the long summer days when everything seemed standstill. She made a small vegetable garden in the barren plot behind the house and had a chicken run on the backyard. The vegetables from the garden and a steady supply of fresh eggs meant she did not have to rely on outside sources most of the time.

Gradually she was getting settled within the small village community; except when Carney became sick and required to visit the local village doctor; Dr Grimshaw, she felt a burden of shame and opprobrium.

Dr Grimshaw had initially displayed great interest in Carney's physique and appearance and almost forcefully referred him to his eugenicist friend; who had fled London to escape the bombings and was living in the same village. Janet and Carney were invited to a room above the local Kingswell Pub where, Dr Grimshaw's friend recorded the distance between Carney's eyes, the width of his forehead, the colour of his eyes and carried out a host of other pseudo-scientific tests, which made Janet remorse and since the encounter; she hated taking her son to the doctor.

It wasn't until hearing about the Holocaust; Janet became fully aware of about how eugenics had been used to pinpoint the Jews; in Hitler's Germany; she regretted for allowing her son to tolerate such mischief by the British champions of the flawed science; who had by that time; had recoiled in horror.

As years passed and the war seemed to be never ending and there was no major air raid in Liverpool for more than a year. Janet decided to move back to Liverpool with 8 year old Carney;

in 1943.They rented a house close to the Albert docks and Carney started school.

But when Janet again become pregnant; the couple could not risk living in Liverpool and decided to move to the Mill town of Manchester. In the summer of 1943; the young Indo-Irish family moved to Levenshulme, Manchester; an area mostly inhabited by Irish immigrants.

CHAPTER 7

In Manchester; Latif and Janet again rented a two up two down terraced house and Latif almost immediately found work at Mellor Mill, in Marple near Stockport. The Mellor Mill was built by Stockport industrialist John Oldknow, in the late eighteenth century; he was England's leading manufacturer of muslin, which had previously only been made in East Bengal, India. The building was six stories high, and the mill was powered by a waterwheel fed by water from the nearby Goyt river diverted into a series of mill ponds. Originally water frames, then throstles ran the Mill. When Latif started work; the Machinery comprised of throstle spindles, manufactured locally. Power was still supplied by the Waterloo wheel, built in 1815 and there were two supplementary Steam Engines.

Latif was new in the trade and his initial duties at the Mill; was arranging for the distribution of raw materials and the return of manufactured goods. This involved a close watch on stock accounts and direct weekly feedback to his Manager through whom fresh supplies were obtained.

Clearly; the post required practical experience in every branch of the cotton industry which Latif lacked. To learn the quickest; Latif, divided six days of long working hours between the spinners, weavers and the packing department.

Eight months later; Latif was transferred to the weaving centre; after his Manager became aware of his family connection; to weavers in Bengal Province; where all his maternal uncles had looms installed at their homes and weaving was their profession. They made fabulous designs using silk threads on cotton saris which were widely used by elite Bengali women; in Calcutta. Soon; Latif's dedication and hard work made him the most efficient of the weavers, with his imaginary skills and in-born talent of weaving; he became the champion weaver within a short time.

Latif's mother; Latifa was from the sleeping village in Jiaganj, on the banks of the Bhagirathi; in Murshidabad district, her father had been an acclaimed weaver and he had a team of people; including all his maternal uncles; together they made time-consuming and labour-intensive hand-made intricate design work on silk; locally known as the Baluchari.

Whenever; Latif visited his maternal grandparents home; mostly in winter; just after the harvest when there were lots of festivities in the village and grand feasts, while all the children were busy playing "Gilli Danda" Indian version of the cricket; he loved watching his grandfather and his team; weaving; transcripting entire tells on a saree; with the Nawab relaxing half seated against a cushion with a drink in his hand; a dancing girl performing at the court with an entire team of musicians aiding her and the most important members of the Nawab's Court watching the spectacle; with minute details of the costumes; sitting positions according to rank; the gifts showered by the Nawab; as explained by his grandfather instantly transporting Latif to the Nawab's Court amongst the audience and he liked it more than the local team of amateur actors playing drama at night; in the village playground.

Then there were other stories; about the Nawab on a hunting spree with his aides; chasing and killing the game, the trees; the excitement; the entire procession, the display of weapons or more important themes like the Nawab working in his Court with his council of ministers and delivering justice to the common man.

Latif; never took his eyes off when his grandfather using the shuttle loom; with the support of others; adjusting the yarn; created fine designs on silk fabrics. However; the clatter of the looms stopped for a while; with the death of his grandfather; until; his youngest uncle started it again.

When Latif was permanently transferred at the weaving section; he soon managed to put the intricate designs; supplied by the archive department in Jacquard format, on fabric; that were sold world- wide.

The manager was responsible for paying the wages, which were extraordinarily low compared to today's standard; unlike many mill workers who were paid via the 'truck system', paid 'in kind' with meat, groceries and fuel from the mill owner's own warehouse where the prices for such goods were way above that in the market place. Latif chose to have his wages paid directly to him and received 1pound 75 Shillings weekly initially but gradually rose to 3 pounds per week.

As wages determined the living standards of Mill workers and with a single child, Latif's family was relatively well off. Far away from the constant agony of being bombed by the enemy; the relative calm also brought happiness within the family.

Next came; Aibrean; meaning the month of April; she was born in the Spring of 1944, on 30 April, the same day Adolf Hitler committed suicide. It was the time when Latif and Janet were still coping with the daily hardships of war and were increasingly wary of the demands and constraints it placed on their daily lives, with nothing to do and nowhere to go except work.

Aibrean was born with a shrill voice and she was never happy; and always crying, however over the year; she grew up as a pretty, plump and flourishing child ... with fine large blue eyes, pretty little mouth and very fine skin, and long black hair, Latif hardly saw her except on Sundays.

The six long years of war at last ended, with the declaration of victory on 8th May 1945, when there were huge celebrations throughout the UK and jubilant crowds came out in the streets, to mark the end of the hardships of the war, as well as the constant fear for the safety of their loved ones who were serving abroad. Janet also took part in a local street party with Carney and Aibrean, where everybody was excited and looked forward for a new start of life with better opportunities for everyone and a welfare state, many were debating the education bill; introduction of the tripartite education system, which people believed will shape the education of disadvantaged working class families children in future and it certainly did so; for Aibrean who despite the personal tragedies and upheavals managed to get admission and studied at the Guildhall School of Music and Drama in London and later at the Munich College for Music and Theatre.

CHAPTER 8

Soon after the war; things were still not improving and there were food shortenings, power cuts and rationing too continued, ordinary people like Latif and Janet were hardly affected by the changes that happened around them; the boys returning home with stories of glory and bravery; making families proud of their achievements and in those families who had lost a son, brother or father there was gloom. Many of the soldiers returned physically or mentally shattered by their experiences of war. For all those who physically fought the war, daily existence had been difficult each day that passed at the battlefield but readjusting to peacetime and family life was proving to be hard too.

In 1946; Janet celebrated Christmas with her family and two aunts; who came from Ireland and they had a traditional first Christmas; after so many years since Janet left Ireland. The same celebrations however continued for years to come until it stopped for ever.

Things such as sweets, meat and butter were still rationed, there were no supermarkets, just the small shops at the corner of the street from where she bought the groceries and the greengrocer's were situated next door to that.

The couple had kept chickens in the back garden since the war and Latif would kill a cockerel ready for the Christmas dinner. It was the only day of the year that they had poultry, so it was very special to everyone.

Janet was a hard working mother, from taking care of her children and being an excellent cook, she managed everything on her own. Carney and Aibrean were very excited and took part in almost everything from Christmas tree decoration to setting up the table. Janet wanted to make sure that everything goes on well with her two Irish aunties and she taught Latif and the children, the best manners.

About two weeks before Christmas, Janet would cook the puddings in the big Burco copper in the kitchen and the smell of cooking added to the excitement and anticipation amongst the children. She also made her own mincemeat, and Carney and Aibrean had to 'have a stir' individually and make a wish. Carney used to go carol singing about a week before Christmas, around the district, singing the proper words and verses to at least one, sometimes two carols at each door and was normally rewarded with a penny, rarely someone gave 3d. It was very rare for anyone to send the children away. On Christmas Eve, Janet took Carney and Aibrean into town, to see Father Christmas at the only department store and then to the Smithfield market where she bought the fruits and nuts.

The children went to bed early, on Christmas eve; hanging clean pillow cases at the head of the bed, ready for Santa to come. In the morning, they wake up early to find pillow cases full of goodies and her aunts arrived the same time, with presents for the children. In the first Christmas Carney got a crystal set radio from one of his grand aunt and he was thrilled.

They had Christmas dinner at 1pm, on the dot, and Latif always set the pudding on fire after dousing it with whisky, a trick he had learnt from Janet, which never ceased to amaze the children.

After the pudding, they all sat down in time to hear the King's speech on the radio.

For tea, Janet always made a Christmas cake and a trifle, with various kinds of sandwiches. She usually used tinned fruit and cream, not real cream of course, but Carnation milk poured over it. After the children had gone to bed, the grown-ups played Monopoly or cards.

CHAPTER 9

Aileen the youngest daughter (ancient Irish name from ail 'noble') arrived into the family, in 1947. The same year; with the independence of India and man- made deformity of the ancient land that once attracted the gaze of the East India Company; as the most opportunistic land, the geo-political situation of South Asia changed permanently and left the entire region to uncertainty, distrust and stringent rivalry between all nations; for generations to come. However; on 15th August 1947 the day India became an independent nation and ceased to be a colony of the United Kingdom; Latif retained his British subject status, which was obtained by virtue of his connection (place and date of his birth; India in 1914) within the Crown's dominions, by being in the UK and was issued with a blue passport as confirmation; of being a British subject.

Unfortunately; Aileen was born with Down syndrome; a variable combination of congenital malformations caused by an abnormal set of chromosomes; trisomy 21. She was mentally retarded and had a congenital heart defect; atrioventricular septal defect causing a bluish tint to her skin and she was breathless on little exertion and had problems feeding and difficulty putting on weight and was also prone to chest infections. Aileen required a major heart surgery to try to repair the defect when she was about 3 months old. The surgery was very complicated and performed by cardiac surgeons at the Great Ormond St Hospital in London when the surgeon had to try to close the two holes (using patches of material) at the same time as; dividing the common inlet valve into separate right and left parts.

Aileen returned home after a month long stay in hospital but she was always sick and every time it cost 2/6d to see a doctor. Fortunately; in 1948 the National Health Service was born and everyone in Britain could then go and see a doctor when they needed to and it was free to everyone at the point of service; it brought a huge relief to Latif and Janet.

Though Latif was normally undemonstrative in his affections for his two older children but he was more open and extrovert with Aileen. He would entertain her with songs and typical tribal dances, he had witnessed as a child, in the nearby Santhal (tribal) village. Aileen felt exciting when pampered by her father.

As Aileen was growing up; living with her complexities; doing many tasks was becoming a challenging experience for her; she struggled with any zip and often put her shoes on the wrong feet, but then she tried to cross her legs and said, 'They're on the right feet now!' She also got frustrated with other tasks easily; particularly if left to eat on her own. Carney and Aibrean loved their younger sister to bits whenever Aileen was upset, they tried their best to make her merry.

To play with; Janet bought wooden toys with different colours for Aileen; to acclimatize her to colours and to help her understand through sensation; she often covered them with velvet, wool, shiny or rough material. Aileen required help with walking, sitting and eating and Janet had to give up her work at the local laundry to look after her youngest daughter.

Aileen started mainstream school at five but being a frequent visitor at the Children's Hospital at Liverpool where a team of cardiologists and surgeons regularly checked on her; she rarely had a chance to go to school.
Aileen died of Pneumonia, on 6 February 1954 at Manchester and laid to rest at the Chorlton Cemetery on the eastern fringes of the city.

Aileen's death had devastating impact on Janet and she slipped into depression and it gradually extended to her social functioning and family life. However; Latif grieved in private, he started working more hours and regularly attended Manchester Central Mosque and Islamic Cultural Centre, at Upper Park Road, Victoria Park; trying to find peace through prayers. The anticipatory grief experienced by Janet and Latif even exacerbated the marital relationship to the point of having huge consequences. The guilt associated with Aileen's death left Janet sexually numbed, she became uninterested in sex, and basically was unable to respond. She being grasped with the feeling that they should not engage in anything pleasurable while their child is dead. Sex for them was no longer an all-encompassing sharing of love, touching, caring, and a very beautiful thing, instead was the cause of the misery.

Unfortunately; Janet and Latif failed to talk to each other about their individual grief experience, there was nobody to help them, instead; they tried to find solace through independent ways and took refuge within their individual religion; ultimately making faulty assumptions and reaching wrong conclusions about each other and failed to understand one another. It was their faiths drifted them apart and the relationship that once flourished and took shape for more than two decades crumbled and no effort was made from either side to mend it.

CHAPTER 10

When minarets' started appearing in the skyline of Britain, particularly in the 1950s and 1960s, as economic hardship in East Pakistan coupled with labour shortages in the UK saw an influx of migrant Bengali workers, most of whom settled down in the Borough of Tower Hamlets; East London but the more adventurous also spread to other parts including Manchester and Birmingham.

Latif's new found interest and association with the Bangladeshi community and inclination towards religion and pretence as if nothing happened, as a mark of spirituality, and believe that God's work for their child on earth was over; made it impossible for him to heal and the inevitable happened. Just before Christmas, Latif left home, leaving Janet, Carney and Aibrean; she was aged 10 years and cried her eyes out for dad.

Janet too was desperate to escape from the relationship and showed no remorse. At night she cried in silent and thought of returning to Ireland with the children. Days later; that Christmas was dull and there was no special dinner. As Carney, Aibrean and Janet sat down for Christmas dinner at 1.00 pm. Aibrean repeatedly went towards the door with the slightest noise from outside; hoping it was her dad but by the evening she was exhausted and went to bed. Carney sat with Janet by the fire and they talked for hours; discussing everything including the prospect of Janet and Aibrean moving to Ireland; to give her the best of the opportunity to sing and her admission into the boarding school, within St Luke's Roman Catholic Monastery. Carney, himself decided to move to Liverpool, the next year to do apprenticeship at the Shipping Company.

Soon Janet and the children got used to the family life without Latif, who never bothered to visit the children. Carney showed no remorse but as Aibrean living in the same surroundings was missing her dad terribly and it was having an impact on her, Janet decided to move to Northern Ireland during Easter, the following year.

Another tragedy struck the family soon; when Mellor Mill caught fire in February 1955, the fire initially started from one of the small cottages close to the mill. Latif was inside when it started and had to exit the building in a rush. He witnessed the entire episode; as the fire spread internally across the building and eventually immense tongues of fire were belching forth from the windows. Higher and higher they leaped and blazed; the building and its environs being encircled with a halo of crimson light. A message was dispatched to Marple and Compstall fire brigade, but by the time they arrived; it was too late to be of any practical service. The spectacle when the fire was at its height was a splendid but awe-inspiring one. Eventually the entire mass of buildings, which covered half an acre in area, was in a gigantic blaze, brilliantly illuminating the district. Huge columns of smoke ascended into the heavens and hung in the form of a dense canopy over the burning building. One by one the floors fell in with a deafening crash and the machinery clanged together like the roar of artillery. Then the roof with one gigantic swoop collapsed, falling through the practically demolished building with a thunderous smash. The mill girls with their shawls over their heads, the children clinging, terrified, to their mother's dresses, and the men who had been striving to render what little assistance there was in their power, were all kept gazing at the burning pile.

Next morning everything was gone except a small portion on the rear side of the building close to the side of the river and Latif returned home drained and devastated with a sense of emptiness and in dire need of mental solace.

Janet heard the news on radio and read the morning newspaper with the vivid description of the horrific fire that destroyed everything that Latif once boast of; though Janet personally had never visited the Mill, but the smell of it through Latif; made it one of the most dearest and known places and she could easily visualize the carnage as it happened through the hour.

When Janet disclosed her plan to the members of the congregation at the St Richard's Catholic Church in Levenshulme, everyone was taken aback in shock. They never wanted to lose Janet and her young daughter; with the most wonderful voice and a choir singer. Aibrean had an inborn talent towards singing and her high pitched voice meant she was the best singer at school and within the Church choir.

After Mellor Mill was destroyed; Latif was gradually drowned into a community and association that considered themselves; entirely alienated from the white population. He was gradually caught in between, his Muslim identity and sense of belonging. His prioritised Muslim identity brought down the conflict with his English family and while he was fighting to shield the memories of the past; his close friend Abdul Quddus advised him to visit his family back home. Though Latif was initially reluctant, repeated persuasion by all members of the Mosque changed his mind and he ultimately decided to do so in the summer of 1956, after twenty six years.

When Latif tried to contact his family in the village, in Bankura district and wrote letters, the response he received from his neighbour was that his family had migrated to East Pakistan, following the religiously based partition that divided the British Indian province of Bengal between India and Pakistan. Predominantly Hindu West Bengal became a province of India, and predominantly Muslim East Bengal became a province of Pakistan. It was dreadful information that Latif could hardly comprehend being grown up as a little boy, on the banks of river Damodar where the beat of the Dhak (drum) during Durga Puja (annual religious festival of the Hindus), the lilting tunes of the folk music, had been indelibly etched into his heart, that was his own native land. He could not recall having witnessed any mistrust or difference between the two communities, except that Lungi (a wraparound worn by men below the waist, usually of chequered cotton) was the hallmark of the Muslims as opposed to Dhoti (a much longer piece of cloth, also worn by men below the waist, but wrapped separately around the two legs, and the tail passed between them and tucked in at the back) worn by Hindus. He clearly remembered having left the village the first time in 1930 with his father's friend; the village chief; a Hindu, he took him to Calcutta and eventually managed to put him in a ship going to England; to quench his thirst to know the world nothing could dissuade him to leave home. Therefore he could not understand the logic of the separation and the stupid decision made by his family to leave everything and move into an alien land with nothing.

Following much effort; Latif at last managed to locate his family, in Pabna, East Pakistan close to India border. Gradually; he started preparing himself for the journey, the reminiscence of the childhood days in the village, in Bankura, India brought back many pleasing and unpleasant memories. He felt a sense of emptiness to leave England, a country, he had been living for 26 years and struggled to overcome a rollercoaster of emotions which was very difficult at times, at last, he dreaded to board the plane from Heathrow for Decca.

This was Latif's first journey by plane and he was scared, though the journey was uneventful as Latif soon got lost in his thoughts; memories of everything shoot passed his mind with the flashback of his life in the alien land which gave him everything; money, knowledge of a new language; English, the language of the elite, in India; that anybody from his family in the last fourteen generations could speak, opportunity to develop his skills as a skilled worker, prestige within his community apart from love, family, joy, beautiful children which he could not keep hold on to and everything was lost; with Latif discarded and thrown back as a trash can within his community; the stereotyped classless community within the fringes of the society who took him as someone of their own flesh and blood, nursed him and healed his wounds and ultimately returning him into the lap of his motherland for a permanent cure.

Latif got puzzled in Decca, he confused East Pakistan with India, having never seen such chaos in the UK, ultimately located his cousin; Ataullah; holding a placard by his name. Travelling to the village in Pabna, his new home was an unknown destination to Latif, there was hardly any conversation between the two but the landscape of East Bengal, with its incredibly green paddy and jute fields and its wide rivers, beels and haors (depressions in which huge water bodies were created by the monsoon rains) stretching away to the horizon, soothed his mind and gave a feel-good feeling.

At home Latif was given a grand welcome; he learnt that his father was killed in the pre partition riots in Calcutta that flared up in August, 1946 after Jinnah's announcement of direct action to achieve a separate state for the Muslims that showed manifestation through violence in the only Muslim League ruled Bengal Province where majority were Muslim; concentrated in the eastern part, but in Calcutta, Hindu's were a majority. But following a rally on the 16th August 1946 at the Calcutta Maidan by the Muslim League as Muslims engaged into direct rioting instigated by none other than the Chief Minister of the state, they had to ultimately pay back as Hindu's stood united irrespective of the political divide and responded with more viciousness. Members of the Hindu Mahasabha; a far-right Hindu nationalist political party that actively took part in the carnage responded immediately, within 72 hours, more than 4,000 people lost their lives and 100,000 residents in the city of Calcutta were left homeless. Violence in Calcutta sparked off further religious riots in the surrounding regions of Noakhali, Bihar, United Province (modern Uttar Pradesh), Punjab, and the North Western Frontier Province and these events sowed the seeds for the eventual Partition of India in 1947.

Latif's family was still living in West Bengal but as large number of Muslims from Eastern India started migrating to East Pakistan, after the Partition that included Muslims from the state of Bihar and Uttar Pradesh, Latif's elder brother decided to move to East Bengal with the rest of the family as thousands of Muslims from neighbouring districts were forcibly ejected from their homes and compelled to move to East Pakistan; the holy land which many across the strata had craved for. Despite not seeing the imminent prospect of eviction, Latif's family managed to buy land from a Hindu family who were hounded by their Muslim neighbours to flee to India from Pabna and started the journey into an alien land hoping that they will manage to tie up with the population without hurdle using the thread of religion. When this family originally from a village in Bankura with a heavy West Bengal accent landed in the middle of East Bengal, everyone in the community was extremely helpful and step an extra foot to help them set foot in the new soil. After seven years of his family's migration when Latif went to East Pakistan, he could hardly recognise the difference between his family members and the local inhabitants; the family having adapted the

East Bengal way totally, the language, the culinary skills, habits and culture. Latif was still sceptical as he could not identify himself with most of their habits and culture; the most prominent was being abusive towards the Hindus and using derogatory language when talking about them, the sense of tolerance and coexistence that Latif witnessed as a child growing up in West Bengal was no longer existent.

Soon he became the centre of attraction of the village and many people started visiting the house daily to hear him speak English with a 'gora' (British) accent.

All his brothers were married with children; Latif was initially hesitant to discuss about his marriage with Janet and about his children but as he disclosed everything to his elder brother who was the principal, of the house, he declared that Latif should get married with a Bengali girl.

Soon Latif was invited to the local mosque when he actually witnessed the damage done by the fire-breathing Moulvi who was capable to inflame passions amongst the faithful and against the infidels.

Latif realized that the mistrust that existed between the communities was bad enough and was fanned to the maximum extent possible by the British in pursuance of their 'divide and rule' policy and the remaining after partition; is being done by religious leaders who continued to fan violence. He felt utterly disgusted and stopped going to the mosque.

As the excitement and enthusiasm died down in just over a month, Latif started feeling lonely and was missing England. However continuous insistence from his elder brother led him to marry Rabeya, a Sylheti girl, almost against his wishes. Latif was still married to Janet and he never liked the girl who was shy and introvert but did spend a couple of nights with her out of compulsion; before returning to England merely two weeks later.

CHAPTER 11

Returning to Manchester felt like being at home, having spent all his savings at home, Latif managed to find work in a local factory and took a rented accommodation. Though initially very busy with his life; he started missing Aibrean and decided to visit the house in Levenshulme; one Saturday morning; when Latif ultimately did so; he was hugely disappointed to find it under lock and key. The next door neighbour; Mrs. Edwards informed him that Janet has moved to Ireland, it was an electrifying shock and Latif for the first time felt the pain of separation from his daughter Aibrean; his tiny little princess with unmanageable curls covering her forehead and her bright blue eyes and her restlessness in all matters, the wonderful voice; she sang the Christmas Carol, her efforts to compete with her elder brother and trying her best to seek Latif's attention all the time. For a moment, Latif felt the necessity to move to Ireland to look for his family but had to restrain himself as he had no address. He felt a sense of loss and returned back to his accommodation defeated and considering him responsible for everything. Latif was finding it hard to navigate the on-going emotional turmoil; soon he started heavy drinking and became a regular visitor at the local Church, attended by Janet, hoping to get some clue about his family.

The self-realization that his enchantment and close association with the recent arrivals from East Pakistan; and his narrow mindset, spoilt his family life, he also regretted visiting his family in East Pakistan after so many years. As days passed, Latif needed distraction to avoid painful feelings; such as loss, incapability, failure, and loneliness but nothing could help him, he tried doing charity work, reading at the local library, chatting at the local pub, gardening in summer, going to the bingo but they all failed miserably.

Latif; discarded contact with his family and so called wife in East Pakistan completely; he also fully alienated himself from the local Bengali speaking Pakistani community; instead he started identifying himself as " an Indian".

Soon he received the news that Rabeya has given birth to a boy; the family has named him Ali. Latif had no contact with Rabeya, she being an illiterate; it was his elder brother who sent all messages concerning Rabeya's pregnancy and child birth.

Though Latif was lazy and seldom wrote to his brother and never bothered to enquire about Rabeya, but he received informative letters regularly from his brother in Bangladesh about his wife and child.

As years passed; Latif's minimal contact with his family in Bangladesh, meant that his wife and child remained a burden on his family who were themselves refugees. Consequently years of neglect, abuse and torment from Latif's extended family impacted on the mental health of Rabeya. As she was losing her mind, forgetting everything and often engaged in self conversation; noticed by all members, she and her child were ultimately returned to her family, in Sylhet in 1962 but Latif was not informed about it.

Following repeated insistence from his brother; Latif again decided to visit Bangladesh for the second time; in January 1965. The journey was uneventful and after reaching home, he found out that his wife and child have moved to Sylhet. The urge to meet his 7 year old boy; compelled Latif to extend his stay with change of plan and his visit to Sylhet. When Latif was there; he lavishly paid for all the expenses of the family; including for the refurbishment of the house; a temporary structure built of corrugated tin. Latif left after a short period of two weeks but within that short time, his 7 year old son, Ali became very close to his father and even learnt a few English words. Latif made arrangements for his schooling at the local primary.

Latif was dissatisfied with his family about their treatment towards his wife and child, however; despite his best intentions; during his second visit too, he could not make any emotional connect with Rabeya. Soon after Latif's departure, it became apparent that Rabeya is pregnant with her second child and it was the biggest hurdle, she failed to overcome with her fragile mental health; going weaker by day. Her family had a lot of problem to sustain the pregnancy as Rabeya went totally insane. Tragically Rabeya died immediately after giving birth to Rois, from septicemia. After their mother died Ali and Rois remained with their maternal family and were raised by them. Soon; Ali became the sole carer of Rois and did everything to give him the best of life and in doing so; he gave up studies at a very young age and starting a job at the market place from age; 12.

After hearing the news about Rabeya's death, Latif felt sad for the boys, he even had a sense of guilt for not trying to connect to her. Rabeya's family soon started insisting that he should take his sons to London to give them a better life. Latif found himself in a situation as having jumped from the frying pan into the fire. With no remedy available; he arranged within Rabeya's family to look after the boys as he couldn't call them over to the UK, the boys being considered illegitimate; he was still married to Janet when they were born. Due to such sense of helplessness; Latif started suffering from low mood and irritability with flashbacks associated with the sense of grief, guilt, anger, and extreme anxiety. He decided to be alone and be happy in his situation and to forget everything; he again resorted to drinking. He discarded all ties with East Pakistan and did not even bother to read the very few letters that reached him.

CHAPTER 12

While Latif was trying his best to adapt to a new life style on his own and erase his past and try to be cheerful and happy with the only recreation of drinking at the local Pub seven days a week; Janet had managed to resettle her life in the picturesque village of Collairne, in Northern Ireland with Aibrean.

Janet never thought to own a home or a motor car nor dreamed of having her children go to university as she interpreted that these were things for people of another class. Having endured extreme hardships as a young girl who was abandoned by her mother at a very young age and grew up at the monastery with the bare minimum necessities, she never focused on what she didn't have because no one in her circle had it either. Therefore; with her very little demands she easily managed to get a house through social housing as hundreds were built immediately after the war, to meet the demands of the people who having experienced the worst of the times and craved for a better life.

As pre war Britain was never to be seen again and things never went back to being quite the same as they were before the outbreak of war. Things changed during this decade because of necessity not choice; many families having lost their sons, husbands, fathers in the war; required financial assistance from the state for sustaining often large families; resulting in UK, becoming a welfare state which was not the scenario before the war; but no matter why; after previously locked doors were opened and once opened they were impossible to close again; as people's demand for better housing, enhanced living standards, improved health care and social care for the elderly and vulnerable rose with time.

Janet also started receiving weekly dole from the local Social Services, as the importance of a family no longer mattered; instead her situation as a single mother was considered more compassionate and she did not have to go through the arduous test of showing her efforts for job seeking. Aibrean got enrolled into the local secondary school situated within the Roman Catholic Monastery where she straight away had the opportunity to have Music lessons and she was in love with it.

Janet also gradually developed regular contact with her two aunts; Guan and Elizabeth settled in Belfast. Both her aunts had a fortune by working in Canada for thirty five years. They had left Ireland, to escape the poverty and managed to find employment as inspectors in Montreal, Canada, before Janet was born and returned only after the war. Both were unmarried with aunty Elizabeth had a long term partner; Alfred who was an Engineer and posted in India; in charge of the construction team responsible to build bridges over the mighty Ganges. Both aunties, Elizabeth and Guan had purchased bungalows in Belfast and Alfred also lived nearby. All three of them had no relative except Janet.

CHAPTER 13

In the next several years as Aibrean's voice got mature and melodious, she gradually got fame and acclamation; her peers insisted that she should take up any better opportunity that comes after completing school.

After the split of her parents and her mother having chosen to have a recluse life in one of the remotest places; Music was all that left to Aibrean and she being attending a very old school had the opportunity to sing and to learn; the piano. She also performed as part of an ensemble. She actively grasped any opportunity that came and at 16, she got the chance to sing at the local pub where she eventually began performing after her 17th birthday and honing her talent.

In 1962 Aibrean caught her first major break when a performance at Belfast radio station yielded a record contract with the American Company Specialty Records producer; Art Dupe to record rock music. Aibrean moved to America the same year but unfortunately her career failed to take off as she hoped it would and she returned to the UK.

While in the UK, Aibrean decided to quit performing rock and committed herself to the ministry and started singing gospel songs. At last; she managed to get admission at the Guildhall School of Music and Drama in London and later at the Munich College for Music and Theatre. In April 1971 she made her operatic debut with the Kent Opera. In 1973, she made her US debut with the Houston Grand Opera, and in 1975 she made her debut with English National Opera (ENO).

Thereafter; Aibrean performed at various operas in Europe and in the US and gained acclamation for her voice. Aibrean became a professor at the Royal College of Music in London. She was appointed Commander of the Order of the British Empire (CBE) in 1993 and Dame Commander of the Order of the British Empire (DBE) in 2011 for her services to music.

But that's only a part of Aibrean's story. Her heartbreaking struggles with her father's identity, mother's loneliness and drunkenness, separation from her brother at a very young age and the abandonment by her father had deep psychological implications on her and lead to ups and downs of her emotional health which always proved a challenge for her to overcome as she was progressing towards stardom. She had always successfully managed to evade questions about her family life and childhood.

In the sleeping fishing village at Collaraine; Aibrean did all the same things as a child as did other children of similar age, irrespective of her dismal family situation that fortunately; did not had any impact on her life in the long run; as it did not matter who her parents were or what they did? Since she found her true aim and tried to fulfill her mission, on the way bounced towards fame; and that was the true significance of her life.

But she was still somewhat different from other children as she loved serenity and enjoyed loneliness; she had a passion for the snow and the cold. In winter; she loved watching snowflakes whirling down in the moonlight; it was like nothing else in the world. It filled her child's soul with some austere; a feeling of loneliness that was never to leave her, it somehow spread a sheen of the snow over the hot, passionate nature of the girl, and gave her a peculiar charm. When the snow covered everything with brightness and purity, she was amazed to look at the lights on the snow and weave fairy tales. Her wild free spirit was already aflame, yearning for something which she knew only in an awakening imagination. She was never indoors, to waste time. There was no one on Drap Road who could skate more swiftly than Aibrean, no one who was so recklessly daring upon a sledge. Even the boys dared not attempt some of the wild feats that Aibrean loved. She loved to throw snowballs at respectable citizens passing by, and fight, with snowballs for ammunition!

Such free spirit; was one of the things which left the deepest imprint upon her character and most affected her; later. When summer time came, and the grass grew green in the vacant lots near the house which were the neighbourhood playgrounds, Aibrean was never quite happy. Then the ugliness of the street and of the houses with their flat faces and blind window eyes were plain to see. She escaped; sitting on the rocks and listening to the sounds of the waves breaking apart continuously.

Aibrean couldn't go more than the rudiments of the academic education, she hated routine and unlike most children she never yielded to the authority; never grew accustomed to the drab lessons and long confining hours.

Years later; she confided during an interview that love of the snow, of cold, of white sweep and swirling snow drops, was to drive her almost mad when she permanently moved to London; where it snowed occasionally and she had no time to enjoy it as authorities raced between themselves to clear it; to avoid disruption to Londoners and to keep the city moving.

Her brother; Carney's intervention at the last moment; immediately before the death of their father in London and taking the dead body to Ireland; to be buried there, upon the insistence of their mother caused deep rift between her and the family; leading to permanent breakdown of relationship as she felt it was a grave injustice done to her father's new family and the children who stood no chance to object to the decision made by Carney.

In recent years, while performing at a show during the summer of 2012, Aibrean lost consciousness. The following September, she suffered a heart attack. She is still visible at all the concerts happening in London.

CHAPTER 14

After Aibrean left Ireland Janet became lonely and desolate, she started visiting her aunts' in Belfast frequently. Following Guan's insistence Janet decided to learn driving, the idea behind was convenient for her to drive to Belfast regularly and support her aunts and Alfred who were unable to do the shopping anymore.

Janet passed her driving test on the 12th attempt in May 1965, almost immediately; aunty Guan gifted her with a Nissan Micra, the latest model that had arrived into the UK, it was ordered at a garage in London and was later transported to Ireland. Janet soon moved to Belfast and regularly took turns to look after the three elderly people. She was busy each day of the week. With Carney and Aibrean seldom visiting her, she had plenty of spare time. Suddenly; aunty Guan's health started going down; her bowel cancer having returned, Janet became busier visiting her at the hospital daily, looking after the house and managing her financial affairs. While at the hospital, aunty Guan called a solicitor and instructed him to probate a will for the property and savings; giving Janet the principal share. Though Janet was unsure of the amount but both her aunties insisted that she should take steps to divorce Latif otherwise; he too will have a share in the inheritance.

Janet frantically contacted her friends and neighbours in Manchester to try to locate Latif or at least get his address; remaining unsuccessful in her attempts. At last; she signed up with a Family Law Solicitors to help her who promised to appoint a private investigator to locate her husband. After waiting for two long years the marriage was finally annulled in 1968, months before aunty Guan's death, she was suffering from dementia towards the end and Janet took all the trouble to look after her; dreaming of the monetary gains. As aunty Guan's mental abilities were declining, she felt vulnerable and was in need of reassurance and support. Janet did everything in her capacity to help aunty Guan retain her sense of identity and feelings of self-worth. But as the decease advanced progressively she gradually lost all her memory and started hallucinating. To Janet's surprise aunt Guan also started talking clearly about her childhood memories particularly in late evenings as they sat down by the fire after tea. Through her revelations Janet managed to acquire substantial information about her maternal family; from a remote fishing village on the western fringes of Ireland and her grandfather's long fishing trips to the Atlantic and the long awaiting of her grandmother in the cliff to get a sight of the sale and the unfortunate storm that swept away everything. What Janet could make out was that her grandfather's rustic boat had perished in the sea during a storm and he did not return. The three young girls and their mother could do nothing but had to leave the fisherman's village where it was impossible for them to sustain and moved inland. Elizabeth was only 2 years old at that time. Janet's grandmother had a miserable life henceforth and Janet's mother; the eldest of the sisters had to do prostitution to maintain the family.

As Guan and Elizabeth reached their teens; provoked by open letters that were very commonly read out during social events encouraging young people to escape poverty, disease, and English oppression and move to America, the land of opportunity and abundance. The girls secretly managed to get hold of a greedy man and boarded a ship destined for America when in their late teens. The journey was terrible; the ship was overcrowded with no proper food and drinking water arrangements, there were not enough toilets and strong stench throughout the ship.

The ship hitting the waters made Guan and Elizabeth extremely excited, but the rough seas made it very difficult for them as they suffered from terrible sea sickness. Extremely weak and frail they landed at New York where they had to undergo a medical examination and then transferred to an almshouse. As soon as permission was granted Guan and Elizabeth started looking for work and despite the discrimination widely prevalent; clearly restricting Irish immigrants to employment, the sisters managed to find work in a mill and rented a basement room in the Manhattan area; ghettoised by Irish migrants living in miserable conditions; with entire families living in one room and due to overcrowding and poor sanitary and plumbing conditions; infectious diseases were frequent. Guan and Elizabeth's room situated in the basement lacked natural light and ventilation and frequently flooded with sewage.

As the two young girls remained clung to each other to tide over the state of affairs in an alien land where they often missed the guidance and love of their mother and elder sister; it was the local Catholic Church; they bonded with like other Irish immigrants.

When the American Catholic Church grew stronger so did the Irish immigrants in America who got assimilated to American life in a two way process without giving up their identity and in turn adapted what was beneficial for them. Guan and Elizabeth enrolled themselves at night school run by the Church. Their efforts paid off as they managed to obtain some qualifications that helped them to move out of the tight-knit urban Irish community of the Northeast to a more elegant and peaceful environment in Canada where life was comparatively better as both the sisters managed to find better jobs.

Gradually the Irish influence in the local Democratic Party in urban centre's with large Irish population became prominent; as the Irish moved towards better prosperity and political prominence, they helped lay the groundwork for today's cultural pluralism in the United States.

In 1913; Guan and Elizabeth left New York and moved to Montreal, Canada and remained there together living in the same apartment and saved as much money as they could and returned to Ireland 33 years later.

After aunty Guan's death; Janet inherited almost £60,000 through sale of her property and from her cash savings. It made a huge difference to all aspects of her life, she became rich instantly. She gave Carney money to purchase a detached house in the posh suburb of Liverpool, referred to by the working class as the 'Bread and Lard

Island' and the folks that lived there were said to be 'All furs coats and no knickers'; assuming that folks like them were all show. Carney had already married a Jewish girl, four years before; who was evacuated to the UK from Holland during the war as a child, but could not be re-united with her family after the war. He and his wife were delighted by Janet's gift.

Prior to receiving the inheritance money; Janet never thought of buying a house, she perceived it as madness and anybody doing so was considered as a class traitor in her eyes. However; Janet wanted to gift her grandson; James the best opportunities; also her opinion changed with money. Still; she never gathered the courage to buy a house for herself until her fortunes changed further in the coming years otherwise she would've spent her entire life; as a tenant.

Janet loved her grandson James; an obnoxiously rude kid, he being pampered by both parents since childhood, everyone in the neighbourhood disliked him for his sudden bursts of anger and selfishness which was gradually making him a recluse but to Janet, James was special, he was the most mischievous child, naughty and hard-headed, and she was the only person who could coax him, it maybe; because they understood each other's feelings and could relate to each other perfectly.

Janet's very simple life, without expectations meant she had the ability to stand up and meet any challenge; she faced in her life. She was a very simple woman but age and the experiences she had witnessed in her own life gave her the ability to pass on important messages easily and James, learned many things from his grandmother, starting from how to deviate his anger and frustration by simple peeling a potato, the war stories, stories about his aunts; Aibrean and Alileen, grandfather, great grand aunties helped him to understand the practical experiences of life; including the meaning of life and death.

According to Janet; watching James growing up given her the chance to live again. The new house bought by Carney in an affluent neighbourhood gave James the opportunity to mingle with children from the different class perceived to be as 'all shows with little humane attachments" by Carney and his family.

Despite such reservations; James behaviour significantly improved as he understood the new lifestyle, he started helping his parents in gardening and housekeeping jobs. Gradually he also learned about the meaning of kindness realising his grandmother's unconditional love for him.

CHAPTER 15

Gradually aunty Elizabeth and her boyfriend; Alfred's health was deteriorating too, Janet remained concerned about her only aunty, everyday in the morning she whisked off to see her; forced her to have breakfast as if she was a little girl and listened to her patiently for two hours sometime more to hear all the complaints about Alfred accusing him of being responsible for even the kitchen bulb wearing off. But the moment Alfred pressed the door bell, Elizabeth was a changed person, the old frail grumpy lady disappeared in the blink of an eye as she gathered all her strength to rise from the armchair and move towards the door to welcome her lover and best friend of nearly a century.

Elizabeth and Alfred met in one of the backstreets in Belfast city centre when Elizabeth was 14 and in high school and Alfred was a mechanical engineering student at Belfast University. Elizabeth always described their first chance encounter as "a meeting of the souls". But before their love story blossomed; poverty forced her to part from her lover as she took the journey to America; in 1905. Soon; Alfred the only son of a British Army Officer; joined the

Engineering division of the British Emperor and was commissioned to India to design and build bridges over the mighty Ganges river; to make it easy for the British Emperor to have easy access in all areas of rebellious Bengal Province.

Though Elizabeth admitted that moving to opposite sides of the world made it impossible for them to get married and have a family but such was the love between them that Elizabeth even at her young age never fancied another man and this continued while living in Canada until her middle age, when she returned to the UK, to be united with Alfred. They of course wrote to each other regularly and shared all the experiences from two extremely different worlds.

Alfred set his foot in the tropical paradise of India when it was just preparing for the final phases of the freedom struggle; majority of Indians despite their class barriers, heavily guarded caste differences and religious segregation were united in one agenda- to get out of the British Emperor. It was however; a matter of debate that different classes had altogether different approaches of the methodology to attain self-rule and had vested interests.

Soon after arrival Alfred was appointed as the chief Engineer to build the Hardinge bridge over river Ganges, in Pabna district of the eastern zone of Bengal; in undivided India, now in Bangladesh. After completion of the project, in 1915, Alfred returned to Calcutta and he was appointed as one of the Engineers to build the cantilever bridge, over the Hooghly River for easy connect between Calcutta with the main railway station, at Howrah' connecting the rest of India. It was a mammoth project involving a large work force and precision work to put in place; the special kind of construction of its kind and Alfred remained busy for sixteen long years, occupied in the project. The bridge was ultimately completed in 1941 and opened to public in 1943.The Howrah Bridge remained the busiest bridge in the world since the time it was opened in 1943 till date.

Alfred often boasted about the workmanship and engineering skills he exhibited while constructing the bridge over Hooghly river; involving Indian workmen who never understood a single word he spoke, all the overseers also hardly understood his heavy Irish accent that often lead to misunderstandings and work being redone at every stage from the foundation to the erection of the cantilever arms and the two suspended halves. Alfred was a perfectionist and never compromised on precision and safety; as if he had foreseen the burden the new Howrah Bridge will take in years to come.

As there was a similar project due to start in Bihar Province, Alfred could not leave India immediately in 1944 but had to linger his stay. He remained in Calcutta, frequently visiting Patna where the bridge was due to be built.

Alfred had a luxurious life in India, he lived in a big bungalow, in the middle of the city waited on by servants, and spending time in posh clubs, attending balls, riding to hounds. He had his chauffer driven car and mingled with the aristocrats on a daily basis at the clubs and in private parties. As an Irishman, Alfred on many a times wandered whether the majority of the Englishmen who saw the work of empire, often assuming great responsibilities and administering vast territories or supervised numerous areas had the capacity to do so fairly.

Though initially peaceful, like in Calcutta, life of many directly involved with the administration of India gradually grew hectic and at times became dangerously unsafe with the immergence of violent extremist groups who identified themselves as freedom fighters and directly attacked British serving officers. Initially the elite in Calcutta were sympathetic to the British but gradually Indians became increasingly opposed being ruled by a foreign power. The march to Independence involved protracted political maneuvering, various reforms, visiting British delegations, much debate and discussion, repressions, mass demonstrations, riots and terrorism. The city, pierced by the Hooghly river, and Alfred's leisurely spend of evenings in the boat on the river, drinking alone remembering his love; Eliza hundreds and thousands of miles away, in the molten glow of the evening sun which had lost all his strength and power except the size was no longer possible due to significant threats; as young men became increasingly wary about any Whiteman and started indiscriminately attacking many, solely to jet past the road to independence, the motive being to scare the white men. Nobody thought about the best reforms and contribution of the English to shape every aspect of Indian life, be it women education, help and support to eliminate the ugly social practices, best efforts to ward off the caste system and in every aspect of life that helped to the development of a Indian middle class who later took control of the independence struggle and all the credit for it.

Due to such absurd threats and incidents happening around, Alfred had to give up his boat-trips but every evening which seemed to be long and unending, he started spending time at his backyard, drinking and walking around in a leisurely pace under the big orange setting sun that resembled the British Emperor; in the decline.

When construction work was in full fledge; to build the Howrah Bridge; while travelling in his car; in the neighbouring city of Howrah to oversee the bolts, prepared at a local factory; a little Indian girl; with pigtails on the roadside kept exhibiting the sign 'V' with her little fingers; as Alfred smiled and made the same gesture, suddenly the girl turned her fingers upside down; symbolizing the end of Victory. Such a gesture would have been indeed humiliating for any British soldier; who were still fighting the War in the Western Front but as a Irish Catholic, the symbolic gesture by the little girl and the smile on her face made Alfred happy, being a proponent of Irish freedom, he too had always wanted the same but it was impossible for him to be open about it.

Alfred witnessed the riots of 1946, in Calcutta that ravaged the city and made it the most dangerous place to live on earth. He lost all the love for the city, he had spent almost three decades as a bachelor and enjoyed the life in Park Street and in the adjoining areas, had few relationships but suddenly everything seemed so meaningless and he just wanted to leave the country and started missing Ireland.

When the Hindus and Muslims in India decided that they could no longer live together and the country was dissected; Alfred's two most notable constructions dedicated and purposefully build for the common people of Bengal was shared between two states. Alfred felt hurt, by everything going around him as his Muslim chauffeur and cook no longer trusted his Hindu gatekeeper, gardener, washman and cleaner. There was mistrust and enmity everywhere. Alfred felt suffocated in the atmosphere of gloom as his bungalow was previously filled with merriment, even his aides were allowed drinking in his presence and there was no antagonism. Alfred previously had never experienced such influence of politics and religion on common people who he knew will remain the same or perhaps become more deprived by the division.

The Second World War had weakened the power of the British Empire and a post-war Labour government in London undermined the dedication to empire and the decision was made by the British government to prepare for the independence of India, resulting in the emergence of two separate nations- Hindu India and Muslim Pakistan and subsequent violence between the three main religious groups; Hindus, Sikhs and Muslims that killed excessively and there is no exact figure available to date on the number of innocent people who lost their lives in the genocide. But the experience and immediate effect of partition on the newly born state and the maternal nation was definitely going to be one of hatred and distrust in the long term which Alfred had little or no problem to understand. In the next twenty five years of his life, Alfred read and heard of countless communal riots that occurred in India since independence whereby it was justifying for Hindus to participate in the killings of Muslims, seen in categorical terms as lovers of Pakistan who should have gone to Pakistan like those who did so; in1947. In contrast to that; the hatred and antagonism towards religious minorities in Pakistan (both east and west) stooped so low that it successfully managed to dwindle the population of non Muslims to non - existent levels; the minorities being subjected to a pogrom by the state and non state actors.

At what time; the rest of the world was experiencing the dreadful war that altered the meanings of the cultural revolution and tore apart the human values previously presumed to be preserved by the Europeans; endorsing and exhibiting tremendous barbarism out- pasting all the difficult times the world had witnessed so far, Elizabeth felt that all is propaganda and find it hard to believe the Nazi brutality. She remained indifferent during the war and simply continued with her routine life; her work schedule being extremely tight, requiring a lot of travelling between the cities in such a huge country; which took a majority of her time. When she was free, being a private person she enjoyed going to the theatre or to the bingo club, all by herself. Despite the success; Elizabeth constantly suffered from low self esteem and a feeling of self loathing as she blamed herself for depriving Alfred of the family, he rightly deserved. Guan was more adventurous and daring; she regularly went out on dates and enjoyed her life apart from her work. But her selfishness and self-centeredness, suffering from narcissistic personality disorder, meant that she lacked a healthy emotional core. She was always driven by a moment-to-moment monitoring of her worth and she was always in love with her own image and saw flaws; as mortal sins, she always wanted to be the centre of attention and believed that her possessions and career "the best" and "special." It was hard for anyone to be around her for long as she had the nasty habit to test others with her controlling, ugly behavior. Therefore all relationships she had ended and Guan always believed that they were not good enough.

Guan retained her character until she died resulting in frequent ugly spats within the few members of the Dempsy family and she was always at loggerheads with Alfred as he refused to play by her terms. Elizabeth on the other hand found boost from the confidence and strength of her sister and to avoid loneliness she never thought of once living separately from Guan.

After completing their work contract both Guan and Elizabeth decided to return to Ireland and moved to Belfast in the summer of 1946. They initially lived together but later parted ways after Alfred returned to Ireland; in 1948.

After 42 years of service, Alfred returned to the United Kingdom in December 1947, initially he bought a two bedroom apartment at Kensington, in Central London. But soon; his life turned as he received the call from Elizabeth to come over to Northern Ireland where Elizabeth and Guan were at last; living separately in their own bungalows.

Alfred took notice of her call and moved to Northern Ireland immediately putting his flat in London on rent.

In Ireland; Alfred initially lived at a Country Club and soon purchased his own apartment close to Elizabeth and Guan's accommodation. However; from 1948 till her death in 1972, Elizabeth had the best of her life as from then on her life was a fairy tale romance with Alfred in which they were never apart. Alfred was often called a "saint" by friends who knew of the constant doting he did on Elizabeth. Every day from 10'oclock in the morning the couple spent the entire day together, having lunch at various places, had different types of leisure activities, entertainments, socialization and then returning to Elizabeth's place at 6 o'clock in the evening to have tea together. Alfred returned to his flat at 9'oclock each night when the pre-booked taxi driver came and beeped his horn. He kissed Elizabeth with the promise to return the next morning and he never failed in his promise; as a true gentleman. On Sunday's the couple spent the entire day at home when they had the Sunday roast.

Both Alfred and Elizabeth were incredibly active individuals; at 65 and 60 they regularly; six days a week went out for lunch at various hotels and after that walked in the town centre for an hour, holding each other's hand. Alfred also regularly played golf and tennis taking Elizabeth with him. Both were members of the riding club and on Saturdays' they went out fishing. Alfred was so keen on fishing that the couple even took fishing trips to Clear Lake, Minnesota, Canada, renting a cabin and went boat fishing.

Regardless of their closeness, Alfred and Elizabeth were 'total opposites' but they just loved being together and of course they would get mad at each other whenever they lived together under the same roof. Alfred was very sociable; he loved doing anything that involved being with people. Elizabeth was quieter but she would support Alfred in whatever he was doing.

Elizabeth was such a perfectionist, a pesky eater that she always nibbled food having had the inherited trend of constipation and piles, to avoid discomfort and bleeding, she basically starved herself; depending mainly on herbal concoctions.

Old age, tiredness and ill health was taking its toll on Elizabeth, she was losing weight fast and despite Janet's concerns about it and trying to boost her appetite with various types of food, she failed to improve. The couple celebrated their 65th anniversary; in April 1972, surrounded by Janet, her children and friends.

But things changed on July 31, 1972 when Elizabeth was hospitalized for a leg injury that within days had grown gravely worse. Come the following Monday, her infection grew worst and she conducted the MRSA bug. Her feeble body was incapable to fight and she soon developed a lung infection when doctors expected her to die.

The time Elizabeth was at the hospital, Alfred visited her every morning at 10 am and spent the entire afternoon sitting and dozing by her bedside so that whenever Elizabeth would open her eyes, she can have a glimpse of him.

Janet also visited Elizabeth everyday and often asked Alfred to leave, as there was nothing much for him to do and Elizabeth could hardly speak or understand events surrounding her, but Alfred was defiant and never listened to, a word she spoke.

Barely a week later; Elizabeth died in the early hours of the morning as she had multi- organ failures, Janet was informed of her death by the ward Nurse and she rushed to the hospital before her body was taken to the morgue. Purposefully

Janet did not inform Alfred immediately not knowing how he will react to the news.

At the hospital, Janet bid farewell to her aunty; Elizabeth who had been fabulous and supportive; helping her to overcome the many challenges and trauma she has had in her life. Deep inside; she really thanked Elizabeth. The nurse handed over Elizabeth's rings; 4 in total all expensive diamond solitaires; gifted by Alfred but the most expensive one given during the last anniversary, a month before was missing. Janet was certain that Elizabeth had five rings in her fingers as she had seen them on her just the last night. However as there was a change in duty and the Nurses who were attending her when she died; were no longer available there was nothing that could be done except lodging a report with the Customer Service Department about lost property.

Janet rushed to Alfred's home as he was ready to leave home to visit Elizabeth, she gave him the news. Alfred though did not overreact but Janet could easily see the black shadow of sorrow and pain covering the octogenarian's face. After spending some time with Alfred; Janet left, promising to arrange for the funeral.

Elizabeth already had a pre-paid Funeral plan with the Funeral directors; only Janet had to run to her bungalow and get the Policy, in hand. After Elizabeth's funeral, it was time to find out about the will. Janet contacted the Solicitors who prepared and probated it. She also kept visiting Alfred who became lonely and was finding it difficult to cope. Suddenly one afternoon; Alfred asked Janet whether he can go and live at Elizabeth's place till the time, he is alive as doing so will ease his pain. Though reluctant; having had plans to quickly sell it off and put the money in the bank, she smiled and nodded to his proposal thinking that he will have the same feeling of boredom after living there alone for a few days and who will live away from home permanently just to be around the belongings of a dead person. Janet also knew that Alfred never spent a night with Elizabeth at the house when she was alive. So according to her; objecting to his wishes might cause a change in his heart and Janet may not receive a single penny from his fortunes after his death.

The biggest surprise came when the Solicitor's agent came to read the will to Janet. Elizabeth had put all her money except a minor share in Alfred's name. There was also clear mention that Alfred can live in her property if he chooses to do so until the time of his death. After Alfred everything except ten thousand pound will be inherited by Janet. Elizabeth made ten thousand pound contribution towards the Children's Charity; Barnardo's Trust; involved in the welfare and providing care to disadvantaged children in the United Kingdom. She being directly involved with the activities of Barnardo's and regularly visited the orphanage run by the trust at Belfast where she found great joy to work with the children, regularly providing gifts during Christmas and she liked taking photographs with the children squeezing in to the frame. A number of those were displayed everywhere at her living room that Janet thought gave her the satisfaction of being close to children an opportunity she had missed in her life.

CHAPTER 16

Soon Alfred moved into Elizabeth's bungalow and Janet as his registered carer visited him every morning to cheer up his soul and to help him with his daily routine. But within weeks after Elizabeth's death, Alfred; who used to be always in a jovial mood, looked gloom and lost every morning. Janet helped him with his breakfast and waited until the Local Council delivered his freshly cooked meal. Alfred always discouraged Janet to put hand to the belongings of Elizabeth, he wanted everything to remain as it was left by her. Many a times; the stubbornness of Alfred made Janet fume inside as the flat was getting dirtier by the day and she could do nothing about it. Elizabeth was a hoarder, there were stacks and stacks of utility bills, bank statements that filled majority of the kitchen cabinets and she could not get rid of them as Alfred did not want her to touch anything. But gradually Alfred's mental health was going down and one morning as Janet entered the flat she had an eerie feeling as she called Alfred's name repeatedly and rushed towards the bedroom but found the bed in an immaculate condition that made Janet more weary, she discovered Alfred lying in the toilet eyes widely open. Immediately; Janet dialed the emergency services and the Paramedics arrived within five minutes but declared him dead. Alfred was taken away by the ambulance and was due for an autopsy to evaluate the reason behind his death.

That night sleeping peels could not help Janet to close her eyes as the death of Alfred marked the end of the generation and she felt lonely and remorse, blaming her for being rude with Alfred; at times. With no siblings and no wider family to share her feelings, Janet repented her decision to marry an alien that severely made her disadvantaged and prevented her from being a part of a wider family. After Alfred's funeral, Janet found out that he had left everything to her, including the flat in London. Janet also had unswerving access to the inheritance left to her by Elizabeth. Within weeks she became stingingly rich and could afford to buy anything of her choice. But Janet's particular mindset prevented her from any luxuries; she however decided to move to the coastal village in western Ireland, the sleeping fishing village on the Atlantic coast from where her maternal family had originated and soon purchased two acre of land just facing the sea. Carney took the ardent job to build the most attractive and eco friendly house for his mother in one corner of the land.

The rest was left as a garden with various flower beds, fruit trees and ornamental plants, tall green trees and a stream running through one corner of it, directly falling into the vast continuous rhythm of the greenish blue Atlantic ocean, where the white water of the stream struggled and fought for acceptance and ultimate amalgamation.

Janet fell in love with the place because of its remote location, distinctive beauty, soon she filled the house with ancient Irish cultural items believing that they are with a magical and mystical energy.

All Janet wanted was to escape into a world of her own creating everything her heart desired, thinking that she will have a perfect life and she didn't need the outside world anymore, thinking that her world will be more exciting as she saw herself in a different time and place. She made few friends locally but nobody was close to her, she only had visitors to see her garden during the summer when it was on full bloom and the fragrance filled the air. Janet always spent time in her beautiful garden to find tranquility and relaxation, where she experienced the sights, sounds and smells and in one corner; facing the sea, she wanted to lay in rest and as years went by she wanted Latif by her side so that she can at least have company all along.

Gradually; over the years men and women from the nearby villages came and spent their entire day in the garden on bright sunny days, noises of children feeling up the area; it was a different experience that Janet enjoyed. But most of the days throughout the year, she was all alone by the sea doing things in her mind.

Though she had no contact with Latif after divorce and was apprehensive to express her thoughts to her children fearing that Aibrean with whom she already had a strained relationship will react negatively to it.

Ultimately on a grey dull morning; when the sea was raging, she wake up with the sound of the phone ringing, it was Carney and he gave the news about Latif, the Nursing superintendent having phoned him after getting his name on Latif's Pension Book. Carney was about to start the journey to London to release the body of his father and make funeral arrangements. Instantly without hesitation, Janet told him to bring his father's body to Ireland to be laid in the private cemetery as she had planned all by herself. Carney was astounded by his mother's demand having thought that it will not have any impact on her. Having proven utterly wrong; he realised that his mother still loved his father and it was destiny that separated them. Carney promised that he will do all the best in his capacity to keep her wish. Carney was sceptical having not aware about his father's new family and step-siblings and whether they will agree to his proposal.

Upon reaching London; Carney met no opposition from his father's new family, they being new in the country and his two other sons; Ali and Rois having no stake in any matter. Ali and Rois fumed at the decision to give a Christian burial to their Muslim father but could do nothing. Carney paid lump sum money to his step-mother, as a pay back before making arrangements to shift Latif's body to Ireland as wanted by his mother.

Aibrean hated what Carney did and she protested even threatening to take him to Court. She also contacted her step family in London and requested her half siblings Ali and Rois to be on her side, unknowing of their individual immigration identities.

In Ireland; Latif was buried at the corner of the garden at Janet's private home. It gave Janet extreme solace that she has won and Latif will only remain close to her in this world and thereafter, nobody will have any right to take him away from the place where he rightfully belongs.

Aibrean however accused Janet of being a merciless woman with only revenge on her mind that provoked her on a destructive path from which there might be no return. Aibrean's already strained relationship with her mother further worsened. Aibrean always claimed that she was born and raised in Collaraine, Ireland. She maintained these fictions throughout her professional life. The story of her alleged Eurasian connections was comprehensively denied by her; throughout her life. The separation of her parents when she was a young girl and her mother's decision to move to Ireland where in an all white school, she was too afraid to reveal her true identity as an Anglo-Indian due to fear of bullying, ultimately closeted away the truth of her life which she could not bring out at any time.

Gradually; Janet's life became extremely lonely and she eventually started disliking any company except Carney and James, instead she loved wandering in her garden in the summer months, looking at the spacious skies, looked upon the amber waves of grain and the purple cliffs rising from the sea. She watched the army of daffodils in her garden swaying their head tirelessly and wandered aimlessly. During the long winter months, majority of her time was spent indoors; she watched the snow covering everything outside by a white sheet.

After Janet's death in 1989, it was revealed that she willed all her property to son, Carney. She was laid to rest side by side with Latif, facing the sea as if these two souls being united once again as they lay peacefully in unmarked graves; separated from the material world; having made the journey together during the most turbulent times when the air was filled with hatred and there was violence everywhere and Janet being the only wife; out of the three with whom Latif had spent the longest and best of his times. It was also her wish to leave the graves unmarked to avoid any disturbance from Latif's wider family in future and she was extremely wary about it.

Soon Janet's home and the garden was sold off to a holiday company and they set up a Country-Park building few cottages beside her original home and a cycle road around the garden which was decorated with rare and special plants and some greenhouses and people came in large numbers to enjoy the beauty of nature, located close to Giants Causeway; it even attracted tourists from mainland UK during summer time.

However; on a windy day; as the sea razed and huge waves pounded the cliff, it became a common belief amongst the visitors to see two figures holding hands and standing facing the sea. Many visitors enquired about the graves with the receptionist who was equally ignorant.

CHAPTER 17

Working hard for ten years in the Curry Industry, with no accommodation costs and free food gave Ali the opportunity to save almost every penny, he earned. His brother; Rois however liked to dress sharp and was always in the hunt for bargains to buy brands, spending money which Ali considered to be a luxury and so not to be encouraged. But given his soft corner for Rois having raised him; as his mother, he never objected to his demands to spend unnecessarily.

In 1990, 10 years after arrival, initially living with the constant fear of deportation due to their fraudulent entry and running away whenever, he saw a Policeman, Ali at last decided to start his own Curry House. Years of work experience in the kitchen that started; as a kitchen porter made him an expert head chef; having acquired all the knowledge which was self taught; watching chefs preparing, self invented Indian curry dishes using their own choice of spices, adding varying degree of sweetness to it to satisfy the British palate. In majority of the restaurants starting from Scotland, Cumbria, Middlesex, Wales and in London where Ali had worked, one thing was sure, if the Englishman liked the taste of the Curry, he came back to the same Restaurant every weekend and celebrated all important days of the year there and a cluster of such regular customers meant; that particular business flourished; all because of the culinary skills of the Chef. So he became the most important person of the Curry House. In majority of the Curry Houses, Chefs' are the owner as it is a risk too big to depend on others for the cooking; particularly whimsical, uneducated lads from remote villages in Bangladesh who just managed to arrive in the UK, by any means and to keep them happy was a struggle for the owner. If the Chef is absent in one weekend due to any reason and the Customers turned unhappy, they will never return and the business ruined.

Himself; a chef who had in the past many years gained reputation amongst the White population at different places in the UK boosted Ali's confidence. He also had the ability to manage the entire small kitchen alone, Ali knew Rois will not be of much help but he was ready. They took on lease a small Cafe Shop in the small town, Helston, in Cornwall, still untouched by Bangladeshi entrepreneurs, otherwise spreading like rodents throughout the UK. Taking advantage of not having any competitor selling the same product, Ali decided to take up the challenge. The shop had two rooms on the first floor which became Ali and Rois's address for the next few years.

The restaurant was opened just before Christmas and prior to that Rois did intense marketing within the small catchment area trying to lure people to have a taste of Indian cuisine and luckily he was successful in his mission.

A number of local residents turned up in the week immediately after the opening and having satisfied with Ali's cooking and Rois' warmth, most of them were happy and promised to return.

In the following months; the brothers turned out to be extremely lucky as people had to wait in queue during the weekends to get in. Their stepbrother; Aklas was with them from the beginning but as Ali needed support in the kitchen and it became necessary to employ a staff, Rois requested a recruitment agent in East London to send a helper for the kitchen.

Helston had a distinctive beauty of its own, a seaside village surrounded by otherworldly landscape; craggy rock formations striated by years of sedimentary build up and salt flats populated by flocks of flamingos for half of the year. Therefore it was not just quaint lodges tucked above the sea line.

Located in an isolated part of Cornwall, made the population retaining their cultural traditions and there was a strong sense of community. Particularly the older generation were very nice to these aliens, many having never stepped outside the town, saw these young Asian men and their exotic food; as a gateway to know the world.

Availability of own accommodation also gave the opportunity for Ali to get married. Almost immediately after the brothers' move, their step-mother found a suitable bride for Ali, a divorcee, originally from Sylhet, in Bangladesh living in a Woman's Refugee in Brick Lane. Ali had no expectations except to get married. After a very humble wedding ceremony at London in the afternoon attended by Ali's step family and few friends, the couple took the bus from Victoria Station and reached Helston by late evening. Rois had already opened the Restaurant and there were few customers on the weekday. Therefore Ali had to immediately rush to the kitchen and the bride; Shefali went upstairs and she seldom came down.

CHAPTER 18

Shefali also had no expectations from her new husband except respect, she having had the experience of a terrible life in the UK. From a remote shadowy village, in the Far East she had made the incredible journey to London after her marriage to her cousin (father's sister's son) unaware of the events due to happen in London. Immediately upon arrival, Shefali started living with her aunt; mother-in-law, uncle; father-in-law, her husband and his five brothers. She was only 18 at that time.

Within days of her arrival, it became apparent to her that her husband already has an English girlfriend and a daughter. He seldom came home; alternatively her five brother-in-laws looked for every opportunity to touch her inappropriately and tried to come close. Her circumstances went from bad to worse in a very short time due to such repeated incidents of advancements by her brother-in-laws. When one of her brother-in-law's tried to enter her bedroom at night, next morning she at last told her aunt and requested her to speak to her sons. Her aunt did not believe her; instead accused her of being a fallen woman and threatened her that if she ever complains again, she will inform the wider family in Bangladesh and sent her back home. Such a threat made Shefali go mute, due to her age and background from a conservative Islamic society; in a rural background where gossips about a woman's character is normally given very heavy weight based on their poor status they enjoy in the society and often become a focal point of a false and primitive concept of family honour, which they are accepted to uphold at the expense of their dignity, moral, health etc. and the list is in exhaustive. Shefali accepted her situation and remained at her marital home, where she was suffering recurrent rapes, physical and verbal abuse, starvation, sleep deprivation, absolute financial destitution and immense mental abuse. Years passed, she became an overstayer and failed to raise the alarm, fearing that she will be deported as her escape route to her homeland was blocked fearing rejection by family and ostracized in the society.

Her perpetrators, knowing too well that under the immigration laws where women who have come over as a spouse; she will have no recourse to public funds and because she had become an overstayer; they scared her with deportation to Bangladesh; repeatedly taunting her to call the

Police, telling her that she will be arrested and returned back home.

The last thing Shefali could do in her capacity was to contact the Police, she being extremely scared of them; having heard stories of terrible atrocities by them at home; forcefully bundling peoples whose visas had expired; into planes and sending them back to their respective countries. Shefali had no intentions to return to her village where the demarcation of a good character from a fallen one was narrow and she would have classified under the second category.

Gradually her situation became similar to a slave labourer, exploited to the extreme level, her human rights breached every moment. Her mental health was gradually deteriorating and with no appropriate medical help, she became worst. When one day, all the family members had left for a wedding; locking Shefali in the house. She crept upstairs to the attic room belonging to her brother-in-law and went outside to the roof. She lost her balance and was hanging from the drain pipe when seeing her in such a position, her neighbour called the emergency services. Eventually the police arrived first and in front of them Shefali lost her grip and fell on the driveway. She sustained life threatening injuries and was immediately rushed to the Hammersmith hospital at the intensive unit.

After regaining consciousness, an interpreter was called and Shefali was informed that she was expecting a child but lost it due to her accident. She also had gruesome internal sexual organ injuries which instigated an instant inquiry considering the criminality involved. Subsequently the social services got involved and after lengthy sessions involving a multiagency team, her story came to light. As Shefali's mental health was still at its low she was transferred to a Mental Health Ward; where it took her six months to recover. After her discharge from hospital; she was transferred to a Woman Refuge Centre in Brick Lane which housed other Bangladeshi women so that she can have companionship. It was while living at the Refugee her marriage proposal was brought by Mrs. Ahmed; a counsellor who was widely known amongst the Bangladeshi community at East London, for her tireless contribution and work to help women in difficult situation, Mrs. Ahmed being involved with Ali's step mother to help her with bereavement after her husband's death.

There is not a shred of doubt that from the very beginning of her life in the UK, her inability to express herself to the authorities due to severe language barriers made Shefali severely disadvantaged, giving opportunity to everyone getting away with the abuse. Unfortunately the immigration laws also helped the perpetrators who believed that she isn't going to get any money or support and that reinforced what they did and gave them more control over her as it is obvious that domestic violence always do not leave proof.

Though she repeatedly missed appointments and there were visible signs of torture on her body but her General Practitioner, a Bangladeshi herself and the Nurse failed to raise the alarm. Of course; Shefali was not aware of what's available in terms of services, she was in a situation where everywhere she went her abuser or a family member - who was colluding in the abuse – was actually going with her, therefore her opportunity to disclose the abuse was severely compromised but she was totally failed by the system, also; there was a real lack of services for women in her position.

After Shefali was rescued, a case was lodged by the Police involving all members of her in-laws. Despite the involvement of the Police and the Social Services, the family never returned Shefali's passport.

As Shefali's case remained unreported during her probationary period and due to this delay it was not possible for her to submit the relevant documents to submit a successful application under the Domestic Violence Rule, a concession given by the former Secretary of State, to enable individuals who came here on spouse visas and have their relationship ended within the visa period due to no other reason but domestic violence to remain here, provided that the individual proves the case by furnishing the specified documents as enlisted in a particular section of the Immigration Directorate Instructions to assess applications made under the Rule.

Attaching such a condition with the Rule which was initially brought with a broad perspective, made it meaningless for majority of South Asian women for whom it was impossible to provide evidence due to reasons unthinkable for people who drew the Rule in the first place. Though the Immigration Directorate Instructions were not inflexible and individual case owners making the decisions had the power to over-ride the prescriptive requirements but none dared to exercise it due to administrative barriers, dearth of understanding of individual cases and fear of losing their well paid jobs, therefore Home

Office in all applications made under the Rule followed a tick mark approach rendering the Rule meaningless.

Though there were concerns amongst the rule makers that the lack of reporting; leading many abused women from South Asia to eventually be deported when their marriages break down and they apply unsuccessfully to stay in the UK, but no action was taken. Home Office rules state that any foreign national whose marriage breaks up within two years because of domestic violence can apply for indefinite leave to remain, but they must have reported the incident at the time to a person in authority - such as a GP or police officer. However; successive figures released by the various agencies showed that more than half the numbers of South Asian brides who say they have been victims of domestic abuse in the UK had to leave the UK after an unsuccessful application; since the Rule came into place because they could not prove that abuse had taken place.

With no possibility of a successful application to be made under the Rules; Mrs. Ahmed being fully aware of Shefali's history in the UK, insisted that Shefali should get married, so that she can regularise her stay based on that.

Shefali had no further expectations in her life; she having passed through so many stumbling blocks in life which she thought was impossible to overcome, though badly physically and mentally ravaged by them, nothing could shake her; it was self reliance that ultimately gave her triumph over her mental health and made her fearless.

Shefali, meaning, Orchid was the name picked by her grandmother, thinking that she will be given the most decorative position by her in-laws. Her marriage within the family of her paternal aunt was thought to be the safest arrangement by her family. However; Shefali had no chance to inform her family about the agony she was enduring while living with her in-laws, after she left the house, her aunt informed everyone back home that she had eloped from home with somebody whose child she was expecting. Such a deliberate rumour; spread amongst the village was impossible to erase at any time and further narrowed Shefali's option concerning relocation to her homeland.

All Shefali wanted was a safe heaven, she had no craving for love and was insensitive to sex. Her job was to take care of everything for Ali and Rois and of course; Aklas who was living in the same accommodation. She cooked, cleaned, pressed the cloths of Rois as Ali never bothered to wear ironed clothes and waited for her husband and brother-in-laws to come upstairs each day at night. But very often felt fast asleep. The only time Ali came close to her and roused her to have sex was in the afternoons; returning upstairs after closing the shop as Rois and Aklas was never there. During other times the couple had very little privacy and with two young brother-in-laws, present in the next room within such a confined space, it was reliving her past experience. Little by little, Shefali started liking Ali who never exerted any kind of force on her but remained indifferent towards her likings; taking care of all her needs.

Shefali gave birth to her daughter; Mahroon, the next year after much complication that almost took her life; the couple was advised to have no more children.

CHAPTER 19

As the Curry business of the brothers was flourishing and they were minting money, given the hard work put together by the three of them, Ali soon had enough money to buy a house. He purchased a six bedroom house at Newport Street; Helston overlooking the bay. It was a beautiful street and the No 5, Ali purchased, stood on a little hill, literally dotted with trees everywhere and with an immaculate lawn at the front, its natural beauty was just more dramatic than others.

The living room downstairs was massive with an enormous window at the front directly facing the sea-front with an ornate carved fireplace, a grand staircase and mosaic-tile floors at the downstairs landing. A skylight fashioned from stained glass, a solarium, and a formal large dining room that were among its other opulent features. Its other distinction was the discovery of the old antique collections of its previous owner who died 19 years ago, that didn't leave the house.

Ali decorated the house with bare minimum furniture and move in with his family and Rois. Aklas refused to come; he was in dire need of freedom. Ali was desperate to have Rois' get married, but with no approval from his side; Ali left it for Rois to decide.

As an outgoing Bangladeshi young man who had adapted to British life perfectly, Rois had many admirers in Brick Lane, London where he travelled regularly each week, driving on his new BMW 3 Series. Everyone knew him as the wealthy bachelor Bangladeshi British lad from Cornwall. Rois always liked making new friends and keep moving on. Nobody knew his past and never talked about his family in the UK. He enjoyed drinking without getting drunk unlike his father and had the mindset to help others; Bangladeshi immigrants living in the rat holes of East London, east of the Roman and medieval walled City of London and north of the River Thames.

Over population, poor education, ghetto of Bangladeshi new arrivals; directly from villages escaping pathetic conditions gave rise to two very distinct classes of Bangladeshi communities within the ghettos. Those who had arrived previously and managed to move out of the Council accommodation through the Food business that was flourishing fast in the UK, as people had by that time developed the taste of the Asian cuisine and were gradually becoming dependent on it across the class barrier. Therefore; whoever had the capability to start a Curry house, anywhere made inordinate gains within a short time; that was the golden era of the Curry business in the UK. However; the Bangladeshi Council tenants of East London, most of them did not lose their flats. Many bought them from the Council, utilizing their spouses showing them being separated from the husbands and therefore had no stake on the husband's fortune. Later; those properties were rented to new arrivals from Bangladesh, most often 15 -20 Bangladeshis sharing a two bedroom house with one toilet paying excess rent as those houses never remained vacant and the immigrants never had the courage to cheat the landlord and even paid due rent after moving out. The landlords made huge profits.

A steep rise in availability of cheap Bangladeshi labour was a boon to the new Bangladeshi entrepreneurs who did not hesitate to exploit those men. And throughout UK, Bangladeshi men started appearing and their contribution to flourish the Curry business was undeniable, without them the Government would have surely lost a large proportion of revenue it had received from the Curry trade.

Rois was sympathetic to those new arrivals and often helped them to find appropriate jobs and move away. His empathy towards the people who had nothing in the UK, of-course made him popular. Soon people started approaching him with all sorts of problems and he became the unelected Community leader; with immense influence on the people, dictating judgments' to solve problems between individuals, helping people to seek state benefit, registration with NHS. As people trusted him wholeheartedly and accepted anything he said. Rois gradually got involved with more serious problems involving the drug peddlers of Brick Lane and their Chinese bosses.

When a 15 year old teenager, of Bangladeshi origin was shot and injured by members of a Chinese Triad gang in Whitechapel area that lead to a series of further attacks and the police were unable to restore calm in the streets, Rois was approached by a beautiful young girl in her mid-twenties to help her family as it was her brother, Dulal who was first attacked.

Rois took personal interest in the matter and his persistent efforts by raising public opinion against such a situation through the local politicians; it reached the political bosses at Whitehall; and Scotland Yard was forced to take action, visible policing into the streets became a reality, to gain the trust of the people and to deter the troublemakers.

After reviving from his injuries Dulal; a troubled teenager was referred to the Social Services. Dulal's father; an 80 year old man was suffering from Cancer and was bedridden. His mother could not speak English. His elder brother; Debal was already in Prison, convicted for illegal possession of narcotics having caught with a stash of marijuana when he was entering the UK, after a visit to Columbia.

As Debal's enemies were keeping constant watch on the family and Dulal too was not safe in the area; having lured to do drug peddling, Rois told Sheela, the sister to move away from East London. It was unthinkable for Sheela who had since the age of 5 lived in Brick Lane. She went to school in the local area and completed her vocational training at the local college, she had never in her life even travelled to London West End. With her father bedridden, mother totally dependent on her for everything and troubled younger brother, taking such a huge decision that would uproot everyone from the community was impossible for her to decide.

However; assurance from Rois and to keep one of her brother's safe and away from the criminal world; Sheela decided to move to a different part of the country. Rois suggested that the family move to Oldham, in Greater Manchester with a large ethnic population of Sylheti Bangladeshis'.

Despite Rois' tireless efforts to relocate Sheela's family successfully, it took almost six months to arrange everything and make the move possible. The family was allocated a council accommodation suitable to the needs of her father and all agencies were informed. Dulal also got admission at the local school.

Keeping in regular contact with each other made Rois and Sheela the best of friends and they eventually fell in love. Sheela had enormous responsibilities on her and marriage was the last thing on her mind. But after meeting Rois, his selfless helping attitude influenced her. Rois' regular frequent visits to Oldham, immediately after the family's move; also helped them to come-closure. Rois and Sheela went shopping, choose furniture, decorated the house together. Nobody knew them in the new town; so there were no raised eyebrows.

On the Valentine's Day, Rois gave Sheela a bouquet of flowers and a note with the five words: "My love for you grows". Sheela was also madly in love but was reluctant to express herself, due to their different religious backgrounds, she from a conservative Hindu family and Rois, a Muslim, she was fearful about the consequences. But slowly all the coyness and hesitation disappeared and the duo were in a serious romantic relationship. Soon their destination shifted from the local restaurants to the enchanting serene stunning valleys of the Pennines around the snake pass that cut across the mountain range and was less than an hour's drive from Oldham. Rois left his car on the roadside at the highest spot and they went for strolling spending hours together, and enjoyed the wonderful feeling of being together, finding similarities between themselves in all matters, Rois also realized that his love for Sheela was not because of who she was, but because of who he was when he was with her.

They had a lot of laughter, playfulness, affection and sexual energy. With no negative traits visible, Sheela asked Rois to convert to her faith to make the relationship real and permanent. Rois had no option and without the knowledge of his big brother; Ali, he converted to Hinduism and was given the new identity; Raj Kumar.

Meanwhile; his long absence from London East End, irked his admirers and they frantically tried to establish contact fearing the inevitable that Rois may have been trapped by the 'Hindu' girl.

Rois did not want to hurt the sentiments of his friends; most of them were staunch Muslims and would not have accepted his religious conversion. He also lacked the courage to tell Ali openly everything, instead maintained that he was helping his friend's family to relocate from London to the North West. However; as the news reached Helston and to Ali that his brother is after a Hindu girl from London, he was unimpressed and initially refused to believe it. He fumed, cursed his brother the first time in his life and vowed to teach him a lesson. Shefali; showed more intellect having learnt from experiences in her own life, she was of opinion that Rois' decision in the matter of his marriage should be respected knowing that Rois' banishment from his life, would make it meaningless to Ali.

Following Rois' return to Helston after a week-long break saw the worst of Ali, as he had an initial outburst on Rois, accusing him of drifting away from his religion, cautioning him about the dangers it will bring as mentioned in the 'Koran' and asked him to start contributing his part of the labour to run the Curry business successfully.

Rois was an agnostic, unlike his elder brother, for whom he had enormous respect, it was impossible for him, to retract and was not worried about any future consequences. Rois always knew about the enormous selfless love, his brother had towards him and he was positive believing that Ali will accept his decisions respectfully. He also cautioned Ali not to discuss his personal matters with employees; the illegal immigrants sent by agencies in East London as it will lead to their boycott and ruining of the business

CHAPTER 20

At last; Ali agreed to accept the relationship, provided Sheela endorses Islam. Rois was nervous to bring such a proposal to her fearing losing her forever. But as normally in the romantic phase, there is a great emphasis on similarities and "sameness"; Rois managed to woo Sheela to undergo a 'fake' conversion just to please his brother, taking advantage of her blind love, promising that he will never stop her from doing anything in the future and only wants this little favour in return.

During Sheela's first visit to Helston; she was astonished, seeing the house, the simplicity of Shefali, Ali and their beautiful daughter; Mehran. Shefali had cooked multiple mouth-watering recipes for the guests and bought beautiful presents for her, gorgeous expensive Asian clothing and a gold necklace.

Soon after, a Moulavi from London arrived who sat in one corner of the room and asked Sheela to repeat verses from the Koran and soon she was declared 'a Muslim' and given the name Ayesha Bibi.

Sheela just nodded to everything that happened as she did not understand a shred of the language and was totally confused. In the evening; she left with Rois and spent the night at a Country Hotel, in Wales and reached home the next afternoon.

Soon; Sheela's father required successive hospital admissions and his health already started declining fast; Rois was always there beside the family, supporting them through all the phases, he also started mingling with people from the local Bangladeshi Community.

Ultimately Rois and Sheela were brave enough to announce their relationship and marriage in front of Sheela's parents; there was little resistance from her parents; her father just nodded his head and her mother knew; that their daughter; Sheela has chosen the right man for her and will definitely be happy with Rois but she will also endure difficulties; when the culture clash will take place.

Unknown to Ali and Shefali, the couple married secretly at the Krishna Temple in Oldham in the morning, the bride was given away to Rois by her younger brother; Dulal, the same afternoon they registered their marriage at the Oldham Registrar Office and left for Helston.

The next afternoon there was a reception party at the restaurant; attended by regular customers; the step-family from London and a few friends of Sheela and Rois from London, Rois having arranged transport for the guests to travel to Helston which was a 5 hour journey by road.

After everything was settled; Ali had hoped that his pampered little brother will take up responsibilities for his wife and will devote time in business. Unknown about the truth, he privately advised Sefali to influence Sheela about the superiority of her newly ordained faith and help her to become a true Muslim.

Though the first few months were smooth and Sheela tried her best to adjust to her new life with the rest of the family members of Rois but constant efforts by her sister-in-law to teach the particular way of life whenever she was in Helston, brought back the memory of what her mother had said; the first time she opened up about the relationship; that getting married to Rois would made life for her bit more sticky than it might otherwise be.

Despite being respectful towards the cultural and religious differences between her and Rois' family, Sheela tried to focus on "sameness", but with the end of the romantic phase, the negative traits of both of them started becoming prominent and it was gradually becoming very stressful for Sheela who hardly had the opportunity to leave home and to escape the company of her pestering sister-in-law.

Little by little Sheela was becoming impatient, authoritative and unresponsive. Her father's condition was deteriorating fast, Rois' was hardly at home and Shefali never allowed her to take up responsibility at home, something she was as used to; since as a little girl.

She was losing respect for Rois and stopped listening to him and started spending more time at Oldham. Sheela's father lost the battle to Cancer in the summer of 1993 and the same time; Sheela left Helston for good.

After the cremation and performance of the rituals, regardless of Rois' request, Sheela refused to go back citing legitimate reasons that she was needed by her mother and younger brother was again steadily moving towards getting into trouble.

Inside her; Sheela knew that it would have been no longer possible for her to lead a double life under the watchful eyes of her sister-in-law and breaking the truth would be disastrous for Rois' future monetary gains.

Rois having used to a family life was finding it hard to live without his wife and wanted to move to Oldham. Seeing him suffering; Ali couldn't oppose him and gave all the support to open a Curry house, at Manchester. He also let go off his most trusted aide; Shan, another Sylheti illegal immigrant from Bangladesh who had arrived into the UK, in 1991 and was working with Ali since that time. Shan learned the skills quickly and became a proficient Curry chef quicker than his contemporaries, giving Ali the opportunity to have weekly breaks. Shan's culinary taste was highly appreciated by many customers who only visited the restaurant on Tuesdays to have a taste of his cooking, the day Ali was off duty.

Giving away such a skilled chef meant a big decision knowing that he can have no more day offs and all responsibility of the kitchen coming on him because Aklas was indolent and uninterested in his job. Ali still let go off Shan, to make the business opened by Rois to become a successful venture.

Ali had full faith on the quality of the food, prepared by Shan who was fast; with the ability to manage a large crowd with little puzzlement. Ali also knew that Rois can never be a chef; and work in front of the burners; sweating for long hours.

Ali came on the opening day of the restaurant keeping the business at Helston closed for the day, the first time since the opening three years before. Ali was content with the set up, chosen by Rois, he had full confidence in him. Sheela's brother; Dulal was also put in the kitchen, to learn the art of cooking from Shan and to keep him away from bad company. Rois was in the front with another Bangladeshi boy as the waiter.

CHAPTER 21

Rois' move to Oldham was aimed to help repair his relationship with Sheela which was strained within a short time immediately after the marriage. Rois' failure to declare his religious identity amongst his close circle saddened Sheela. Also forcing her to act in a manner to which she could never identify; broke her heart. Sheela always admitted that Rois' immediate family members were extremely good human beings but the culture clash that separated her from them was too big to be filled at any time.

As a young couple; Rois and Sheela courageously struggled but choose to stay together for a variety of reasons, their religious and family values, wanting to keep the family together as Sheela was already expecting their first child.

Therefore; they decided to go slowly; giving opportunity for lasting healing to their relationship and to adjust to their situation they needed time; by putting their time and energy into other activities and interest.

Sheela finding employment at the local primary school meant that they found two alternative worlds' of their own. Sheela was busy with her school, child and family while Rois hardly found time outside his business and community work.

He was determined to make the business a success and at the same time, it was impossible for him to give up his inherent quality to get involve with his community where majority were uninformed and required assistance to have access to the multiple state benefits vital to their survival.

It is a fact; that majority of the South Asian first generation migrants who came after the closure of the Mills; did not have the skills to climb the job ladder. However; the Curry industry gave majority of these people the opportunity to earn a tax free wage. Therefore relying on benefits despite being employed; made these benefit cheats; 'a distinctive rich class' by having double the income from their white English counterparts. The money was systematically siphoned to their country of origin, to build palatial buildings in remote villages, with no electricity or running water.

Rois was aware of everything but still could not stop helping those who wanted it, gradually he was becoming popular amongst; Bangladeshis', in Oldham, Rochdale, Manchester area, people started flocking in his restaurant, transforming it, into an advice centre, during the afternoons.

Gradually; given his ability to speak English and Sylheti fluently and deep association with the community, he became a prominent member and a community leader. Rois started solving various problems encountered by the Bangladeshi community; on a self proclaimed People's court, without the intervention of the authorities. Giving advices and dictates and solving the multidimensional complex problems that were impossible for the authorities to solve due to their weird nature and outside the framework of the UK legal system. As his fame of popularity reached its peak, he came under the scanner of the Political leaders, was approached by the local Bangladeshi Councillor, to join his party. Rois joined the Party as an ordinary member but merely a year after; with the vacant of the seat at Oldham Council; he was offered the same considering the rise in ethnic Bangladeshi population in the area and Rois' popularity and the importance of obtaining the entire South Asian vote share to defeat the opponents.

Rois defeated his immediate opponent with a considerable margin and he maintained similar lead and retained the seat in the next 10 years, before becoming the Mayor of Manchester, in 2004.

At his inaugural ceremony at the Manchester Cathedral amongst the attended guests was Aibrean, invited by the Archbishop of Manchester, at 60, she still had the most melodious voice and attracted the attention of the guests.

Meeting with Rois; her step brother, almost 20 years junior to her, was very exciting for Rois. Aibrean on the other hand; showed little enthusiasm. Rois and Aibrean had a private chat after the ceremony when for the first time; Rois became aware of the actual burial place of their father, in Ireland. He expressed his desire to visit his father's grave and invited Aibrean to visit his family at Oldham.

That evening; Aibrean took a taxi as she could not resist the desire to visit Levenshulme and St Richards Roman Catholic Church where she first begun singing, as a little girl; in the fifties. The taxi driver took her to the street where to her horror, Aibrean discovered that all the houses which was once a part of a vibrant community were undergoing demolition to give way for a huge supermarket to serve the people and the Church building, where she first began singing, is now in a shameful state of neglect and decay and a 'For Sale' board hanging on it.

CHAPTER 22

St Richards Church stood in a spacious churchyard with burials; at the corner of Waterloo Road and Alexandra Road. The churchyard surrounded by a low stone wall pierced by good iron gates, and surrounded by sycamore and elm trees. The original building was constructed in the early 1700 but the tower was added more than 100 years later. Aibrean remembered everything, how she run to father Dever whenever she had a shred of doubt in her mind, the tightly knitted community, Mrs. Hansen, Ms Louise and many more elderly ladies with heavy Irish accents, her secret daily prayers sitting in the corner just beside alter and praying for her father to come back home; something that never happened. It was in this very place, she first started singing at the choir and everyone cheering her on Sundays, using the same praise again and again. Aibrean wanted to get inside and see the place for the last time before it became a victim of the council inspired vandalism and replacement of its feature and the systematic destruction of the art inside; that has inspired Aibrean as she looked up to the ceiling and sang.

Carefully she managed to get inside the backyard through a gap in the wall, she walked up-to the back, being aware of the secret entrance, it took her sometime to clear up the weeds before the black tar painted door appeared and after much effort, Aibrean managed to open it with a loud cracking sound and she entered carefully, as Aibrean went past the dark passage disturbing the inhabitants, she had an eerie feeling.

Ultimately Aibrean reached the pantry room and walking down the corridor she reached the main Church hall, the high walls with large arched windows covered in stained glass painted with baby Jesus in his mother's arm are still there, there were cracks all over the walls and on the roof, causing water to leak down over the fragile frescoes and the mosaics, discoloring most of them. The moisture entering from below increased humidity within the hall, giving rise to a distinctive pungent smell. The air inside was still, the gloom in the empty hall was like time mourning its own passage, a surrender to dust, to dampness and to death. It was the indifference of a terminal patient to a visitor who brings no hope but stands by the bed. As Aibrean looked around, the archangels, Virgin Mother, Jesus, the saints are all weeping as they looked at her. Suddenly a soft ray of penetrating light from one of the windows awakened Aibrean and she moved few steps forward, immediately the mole-infested floorboard she was standing on collapsed.

Aibrean searched for strong floorboards as she moved towards alter, her attention drawn towards the picture board with black and white photographs pinned to it. As she cleared off the dust from top, she struggled to look for a familiar face. Her attention immediately drawn towards a frame with a group of small children squeezed in with a tall man. She immediately remembered, she was right there, the photo taken on Christmas Eve, with Father Dever, taken by a local newspaper photographer; just before Father Dever handed over Christmas presents to everyone in the photograph. Her memory; raced to remember the vibrant community, around the Church. They met in the laundry for washing and gossiping, in the gym for fitness without a fee, they took part in parades and celebrated all the joys of life together- she remembered growing up there with her mother, father and big brother, never understanding her mother's decision to move to Ireland where she could never reveal her true identity.

As Aibrean decided to leave the Church building, she carefully minded her steps towards the exit following the same route, loathed with the idea that soon everything will disappear or encroached upon by the migrants, who will probably transform history into a warehouse that detested her mouth. That was her first and last visit to Manchester after more than four decades.

CHAPTER 23

Over the years Rois; became more involved with the local community directly engaging with the youth, born and bred in the UK, inclined towards extremism by the false propaganda and notion that it is planned conspiracy by America and the West to destroy the Muslim world as more and more Muslim countries started to run into chaos and engaged in heavy infighting, millions were made homeless and thousands including children lost their lives.

As violence sore and the extreme sufferings of fellow Muslims caused by Muslims became a reality, the disgruntled state school educated young generation of the South Asian immigrant population in the UK, whose parents or grandparents had initially worked hard to build a life in the UK, were easily attracted towards extremism and started harnessing innovative ideas to attack the Western culture and values; firmly based on the essence of democracy.

Rois was certain that the disengagement of the parents, mostly surviving on benefits and tax-cheaters; caused majority of the young generation, mostly those; in trouble with the authorities, indoctrinated with the idea of vile of the western culture and society by the orthodox, radicals shipped into the country from the hostile middle east and north Africa.

Such was the impact on children from lower middle class South Asian parents; who had happily participated in all aspects of British life in the late sixties and early seventies and endured the harshest racism, yet never thought of harming the country; were now easily lured to a life based on the principals of violence, whether committed within or outside, killing innocent civilians.

As Rois started working tirelessly to improve community relations in Greater Manchester, his dedicated efforts and direct involvement helped many parents to bring back their children to the society and community, they belonged.

Also his collaboration and assistance to the authorities to keep Britain safe from any nefarious activity of stray disgruntled South Asian population was enormous and highly regarded.

The timid little orphan from the remote hinterland in Bangladesh; easily stepped the ladder of fame; as he was becoming a popular face, in social, political and official gatherings. The self-motivated journey; linked to the wounds of his childhood, to help the disadvantaged community that began in London, got fulfillment in the North West where he rose above the boundary and he became a popular name across community barriers.

Also with the passage of time; as the children moved to High School, Rois and Sheela's tumultuous relationship underwent growth and healing as they both understood that much of the relationship conflict lies in the way they learned to cope with life's stresses as a child and during teenage years, unknowingly replicating some of the painful experiences they had experienced in early life--thus creating the pain to each other. As they realized the wonderful, frustrating, complexities of committed love along their journey, they again came closer to each other, understanding and learning a lot about each other and the relationship slowly started growing, healing the frustrations and hurts that were driving them apart.

Rois' contribution towards Sheela's family was also undeniable, he shaped and channelized the distorted life of her two brothers, who found a steady income source and being kept too busy at the restaurant, hardly gave them time, to engage in any other business.

Ultimately; after many years of marriage; Rois and Sheela found marital and relationship satisfaction with each other; being in realistic love, grounded in understanding, healing and growth.

As Lord Mayor of Manchester; Rois was invited to visit the Mellor Mill, in Stockport as a joint initiative was proposed by Manchester and Stockport City Council to transform it into a Museum, in private-public partnership. When Rois visited Mellor Mill, the work place of his father, after almost 50 years, it was in a dilapidated condition, being used in parts for stabling or for minor industrial purposes.

As the team went to explore the upper floor of the building, they found a great number of letters, papers, account books, and other business records of every kind and size, covering the whole floor of a large room and partly hidden from sight by several inches of dust and debris.

One of the Council employees picked up a small piece of paper; burnt in the corner and removed the dust and handed over to Rois, telling "mid-twentieth century weavers' pay-tickets", Rois grabbed it without hesitation and put it in his pocket. To all others within the team; the appearance of the records that had laid there for almost half a century had no apparent significance, except Rois who felt connected to the place, trying to place his father, busy working, in the dusty, gloomy environment under hazardous conditions.

The fire made it lost many windows and roof tiles; the building was in need of extensive repair and required appropriate funding. A committee was set up under the chairmanship of Rois to have an oversight, on all the work, in the project. It took months to clear up the debris to reach the original findings that included the business records of Mellor Mill and list of employees where Rois found the details of his father and his residential address, the name of his next of kin and number of children. Also; within the records were included the fragmentary time books, wage sheets and personal records of employees of two other Businesses owned by the owner of Mellor Mill, previous to his move to Stockport.

Rois as Lord Mayor of Manchester and Chairman of the Mill Museum Committee did all the best in his capacity to accelerate the project, still it took almost two years for completion. Mellor Mill Museum was opened to the public, in the summer of 2007. Being so deeply involved in the project, Rois sent a personal invitation to Aibrean but unfortunately she could not make it due to ill health.

CHAPTER 24

Shan started working for Rois from the time, he parted from his brother and started his independent Curry business, in Manchester. Shan, an illiterate, Sylheti had arrived into the UK, in 1991, using a Bangladeshi passport. Immediately upon arrival he managed to open a bank account and applied for a Provincial Driving License. After six months; Shan started window shopping, one of the solicitors, in Whitechapel gave him the idea that the only successful possible claim for asylum from his country of origin; could be based on his ethnicity, if he declares himself as a 'Bihari'. But applying common sense; to succeed under the premise, Shan was required to know 'Hindi' the language of the Biharis' but he was unable to utter a single 'Hindi' word.

He was told that asylum was an easy-ride, following the normal timescale; it will take five to eight years, to complete the entire process, before one became appeal rights exhausted. The bonus was after six months, asylum seekers were issued with work permission, so there was no barrier to earn money. Also; with the passage of time, many have their circumstances change through genuine and fake marriages, going into hiding; working in remote Curry businesses; in villages till they managed to spent a specific time period that qualified them, to apply under the rules. The simple truth was; poor farmers, landless workers from the Asian subcontinent, only wanted to stay in the UK for financial gains and Shan was no exception.

Originally from a landless family, living in the banks of river Jamuna, Shan was from a disadvantageous background, though an illiterate, he was hardworking, intelligent and a good learner.

Shan was quick to learn the art of cooking from his master; Ali who took years to learn the same cooking which neither Ali nor Shan had ever tasted before, to suite the palate of White British customers. With lot of honey or sugar going in all the dishes, they were sweet as a pie but the mixture of Indian spices, gave it taste and the garnishing with fresh tomatoes and coriander leaves brought colour. The trick of becoming a good chef, in the curry industry was to understand the varying degree of sweetness and hotness liked by individual customers and to remember the same, so that the same folks came back every weekend after a night out and Shan had a very good memory, he remembered every regular customer's choice and never failed to satisfy them.

Years of experience cooking the same dishes with the same ingredients, standing in the same position made him very fast and nobody could beat him. At times; when the restaurant was filled with almost hundred customers, Shan worked superfast and managed the cooking singlehanded.

Gradually; over the years, it became Shan's show during weekends to run the business as Rois was busy shaping his political ambitions and mending the relationship with his wife and Rois' two brother-in-laws, managed the front and struggled to keep account of the sales.

As fame spread white people queued up during the weekends to have a taste of the curry. Shan though lowly paid by his boss was still satisfied with his salary and was minting money as he had zero expenses. Whatever he earned; was tax free and saving.

CHAPTER 25

Just before Christmas, on a busy Friday night, Immigration Officers from the local enforcement office, after a tip off, raided Rois' restaurant, Shan was arrested for not having a valid Immigration ID and taken for questioning.

Extremely shaken by the incident; Shan lost his speech and was unable to utter a word as he was taken away in the van, to a detention centre. He remembered the threat by a British born Sylheti boy who came to work as a kitchen porter but had a fight with him. Shan was crying his eyes out as suddenly he saw the flood waters of Meghna breaking the embankments and water rushing into their village and engulfing everything what was dry land, a moment before. His hallucination was interrupted as the van entered the gates of the high walled detention centre and he was taken out.

Shan had never been to Prison, in his life having heard all the stories about bullying, fighting, drug trafficking and gay relationships within it from Rois' brother-in-laws. He was terrified thinking that he had ended up in Prison. The tall guards in their White Shirts and Black Trousers had grin faces and were walking straight. Shan being directly brought from the restaurant kitchen, he smelt foul that filled up the air, immediately he was handed over a set of clothes and asked to change.

After registering his details, Shan was allocated a sharing room, a small 4mX4m cubicle with a shower that he had to share with another detainee.

After getting his keys, Shan moved to his room, to his surprise, the man occupying the other bed was 23 year old, Eklas Miah from Sylhet. Eklas told him that he had been in detention, since he was discovered in the back of a lorry, in Dover, three months before and though the authorities wanted him to leave the detention facility but he is unwilling to go out to avoid the smuggler who brought him into the country.

Eklas was God's gift to Shan, with no language barrier between them, within one night he acquired all the knowledge about the detention centre and assurance that it is not a prison but like a hostel where the only barrier is not have the freedom to walk out of the facility and that helps many to escape a degrading life outside of the premises.

Eklas also gave him assurance to help with his immigration matters. Since; Shan had initially submitted a postal application for asylum more than 10 years before and lost contact with the Home Office, he was in a perilous situation. As Shan had no knowledge about anything related to the 'Bihari' issue, in Bangladesh, Eklas told him to change his story and apply for political asylum.

Dulal contacted Shan the next morning and assured him with all the help; he had by Monday managed to hire a private representative; Ms Sen to deal with Shan's immigration matters. Shan had been extremely shaken by the turn of events; his detention, the shouting of the Immigration Officers who detained him at Manchester and he didn't know what to say. However; Ms Sen instructed him to remain stick to his earlier claim, 'as a Bihari' from Bangladesh, rejecting his idea of political asylum, in the entirety.

She assured Shan that she will prepare his statement and discuss the same with him in his native language. But Shan was still feeling nervous about facing the interview on his own, he requested Ms Sen to be present during the process. Shan's story was remodeled as 'an orphan', he was abducted from the 'Bihari refugee camp' in Dhaka, at a very young age;

when he was about 10 years old and taken to Sylhet and sold to a landlord. He worked as a bonded labour with his master until the time, he was identified by the local Police as 'a Bihari' following a disturbance during which an Awami League supporter was murdered and the man responsible for the murder was believed to be 'a Bihari', the most obvious enemy of Awami League members and supporters; since Biharis' were believed to be against the freedom struggle having colluded with the Pakistanis and collaborated with them to commit heinous crimes.

As Police started combing the villages looking for anyone with 'a Bihari' link, Shan became fearful, he being the only 'Bihari' known to locals and he fled to neighbouring India, the land of his ancestors.

Entering India; through Silchar, Assam; as a young man, Shan tried to settle down in lower Assam, working as a 'hired labourer' but due to extreme communal tensions, in the area he ultimately moved to Calcutta.

After spending months in Calcutta, sleeping rough and working as a daily labourer, he ultimately managed to leave the country, on a fake Indian passport and flew to Moscow, from where he made the arduous journey across land arriving into the UK, in 1991. His journey; been planned, funded and guided by the agent and his men, 'people traffickers' and paid off by a sponsor in Calcutta on the condition that he will have to donate one of his kidneys, to an ailing Indian businessman, in the UK. There were elaborate medical tests conducted on him in Calcutta; prior to his journey before his sponsor paid the agent. Shan also maintained that he had never been to school and is illiterate.

Based on the above submissions made on Shan's behalf highlighting his trafficking history and ethnicity, as 'a Bihari', Home Office booked a 'Hindi' interpreter to assist Shan without looking into the details of the case. However; this mistake hugely favoured Shan to roll over the interview process with assistance from his representative.

His representative, a young, smart, Indian Bengali girl, Ms Sen arrived just before the interview, she had prepared Shan's case and asked him not to deviate from his statement. The assurance from her; helped Shan who almost had a nervous breakdown, to come back to his feet.

Mr S J Rowland, the most witty and impolite officer, came to the interview room accompanied by the Hindi interpreter. Ms Sen, did not object to the use of a Hindi interpreter as it gave her the freedom to give words to the mouth of Shan and act as a negotiator between her client and Home Office interpreter.

Throughout the three and half hour long interview; Rowland was extremely harsh and asked the most difficult questions. He doubted his 'Bihari' claim from the onset and threatened to remove him to Bangladesh, almost shouting at him. Ms Sen politely requested Mr. Rowland not to intimidate her client, as he is an asylum seeker and such an attitude by a representative of the Secretary of State, is against the Convention guidelines.

Mr. Rowland though irked by such interventions still insisted that Shan is not what he is saying. After a short break, suddenly Mr. Rowland asked Shan to name few important buildings in Calcutta. Looking towards the interpreter, Ms Sen immediately told Shan, in Bengali that he slept rough under the 'Monument' and requested the interpreter to translate the same for Mr. Rowland.

Rowland was confused from the answers, he was getting from Mr. Shan, in response to ethnicity; he replied 'Bihari', in response to religion, he replied 'Muslim' and in response to occupation; he replied 'slavery'.

As Shan was adamant with his claim, in front of his legal representatives and Ms Sen's mere presence gave him enormous moral strength and support, there was little in Mr. Rowland's capacity to do, in the matter. Moreover; the authorities were already severely disadvantaged, in the case, having unable to conduct the asylum interview of Shan, in 10 years. Ms Sen; in her submissions gave stress to this particular point maintaining that as an 'illiterate Bihari refugee,' it is inappropriate to ask elaborate questions to Shan, in relation to his asylum claim after 10 years as this approach could damage his credibility. Ms Sen was careful; she didn't want to mess-up the chances of Shan, knowing too well that the Home Office was already in the back-seat, due to the inordinate delay on their part to conduct the initial interview process or produce letters that they have made attempts to contact Mr. Shan previously.

Also; the gruesome trafficking history of Shan, added colour to his case and Shan gave consent to divulge further information in regard to his trafficking history and organ donation scam, if required by the Home Office during further investigations.

Soon after the interview, Ms Sen submitted a bail application for Shan and given the complexity of the case, it was almost immediately approved by the Chief Immigration Officer, the same night, at around 8 PM, Shan was released with the travel ticket to travel to Manchester.

Shan returned to Manchester reaching almost at midnight and straight way went to the restaurant and ran into kitchen; finding everything in a mess as the two brothers; Dulal and Dilip struggled to manage the cooking.

The cookers were splattered with oil and grease and all the various spice mixtures were almost empty, the freezer was almost empty too, the floor was sticky and the bins were full. Whatever; the condition Shan just loved to be back and went to his room upstairs.

CHAPTER 26

Since; his release from detention, Shan made up his mind to pursue his case actively and he remained in contact with his representatives who regularly reminded the Home Office about his pending case. Meanwhile; as hundreds of thousands of old unresolved cases piled up in the Home Office, the Home Secretary, in a bid to stir-up the sensitive immigration issue, declared to Parliament, his intentions to clear up the cases; to end the backlog, either grant individual applicants; indefinite leave to remain in the UK thereby allowing them to remain here forever or remove them from the UK.

But removal being a highly complicated process; prior to which the Home Office is obliged to take into account all relevant factors; including whether the person, removed to a particular country would be allowed entry. However; the removal process being independent of any application for leave to remain or a claim for international protection; officials dealing with the cases initially often displayed insensitivity and never take into account; the barrier to removal of an individual while considering the case.

Such; an approach of course meant; leading to huge backlogs and impossibility to clear up the mess; even with large recruitment of staffs. Though; an initial application except for a claim for international protection was refused promptly; the asylum cases took almost two and half years; after which it started the legal journey moving in snail pace through the various tires of the Judicial system; that gave ample time to people; strengthening their ties and helping with the economy; as the Curry industry and others flourished staffed by people; who had lost their right to be in the UK.

Also; the implementation of the human rights act; in 2000 made it mandatory for each and every individuals who are in the UK, to have their human rights considered while making a decision.

Therefore; individuals who had their applications and claims refused years before but still were in the UK, had their cases reviewed under the human rights act and whenever Home Office refused to accept that there will be a violation of human rights upon removal the decision triggered another chain of challenges that had the potential of ending up at the European Court of Human Rights; the ultimate authority to decide whose wrong and whose right. Also application from all member state countries to one body meant delay was inevitable and again the process was outreach of the Home Office.

Though Shan had never received any initial decision on his application but soon he received a standard letter from the Home Office confirming that his case is in the backlog of cases waiting for consideration, requesting further documents.

Shan was waiting for the opportunity; he submitted all the documents; related to his work history; recipient of the Curry Award for successive years as the Best Curry Chef of North West, his financial history and education history; commensurate to his training and NVQ qualifications; he having underwent baking and roasting diploma at a Private College following insistence from Rois who arranged everything.

Referrals from notable members of the community and his regular customers also accompanied the documents; of course many of them mentioned about the hotchpotch on the day Shan was taken away by Immigration Officials from the Restaurant; everyone wanted Shan.

Request was also made on Shan's behalf to consider his case in the same way as a new application giving an anxious scrutiny to his case as a 'Bihari' who left Bangladesh as a child, have no permanent address there and have no family ties and fears being a victim of indiscriminate violence as witnessed by him throughout his childhood, the deteriorating social, political and economic turmoil Bangladesh has undergone while he was in the UK also taking into account his human rights factors.

Shan's representatives argued that it is wrong and arguably, in some circumstances, contrary to the provisions of the European Convention on Human Rights, that people like Shan who has already spent a significant part of his life in the UK and has completely adopted himself into the English society and waited for such a long period for a decision on such an important matter as having to leave the country in which he has been living for more than the last 14 years to a country where he fears torture. Because; the Home Office was randomly refusing the old cases upon review with no right of appeal, Shan's representatives further submitted that; when the Home Office alleges that a person who is a failed asylum seeker there is no judicial forum in which this can be contested, regardless of how long the person has lived here or however strong private/family or compassionate reasons there may be which gives rise to conspicuous unfairness and an abuse of power.

Ms Sen also accused the Home Office of having failed to recognize the fact that there are a myriad of human rights issues in Bangladesh where 'Biharis' are suffering since the last three decades and the successive governments in Bangladesh has failed to fulfill its obligations under national and international law with regard to the treatment of 'Biharis' left stranded in the country; leading to this particular group of people being subjected to social alienation, deprivation, illegal detention and systematic persecution. Moreover; she maintained that the denationalization of 'Biharis' by Pakistan has made them de facto stateless refugees for whom there are special provisions within the 1951 Geneva Convention. That; Bangladesh having failed to ensure that abuses by state and private agents are effectively and independently investigated and perpetrators brought to justice and instead those who violate human rights are often given impunity by the state. Therefore; the challenges faced by victims and their relatives in pursuing legal avenues for accountability of the human rights abuses perpetrated there indicates the impunity enjoyed by the security agencies and the near total failure of Bangladesh's judicial and state institutions. It was submitted to consider his case under the legacy case resolution program and granting him indefinite leave to remain in the UK.

While the legacy framework set up by the then Home Secretary became active and functional; they started considering the cases with an aim to clear the backlog of hundreds and thousands of age old cases which remained stacked in the Home Office shelves. Shan was extremely lucky to be one of them. Given the peculiarity and the delay related to his case, based on his interview and subsequent documentation provided to the Home Office, he was granted indefinite leave to remain.

Shan was lucky to have been granted leave in time as the legacy casework changed overtime, due to political constrains and individuals' who failed to take advantage of the announcement in time, fell for refusal without any reasoning under the premise that it was not an amnesty and therefore single applicant's had little room to succeed; by rowing through it. Also; the entire team was dismantled and restructured few times but as individuals whose cases were refused could not be removed from the UK, the backlog which the Home Office set up to clear started building up again.

CHAPTER 27

Once granted leave, Shan was ecstatic, his joy was boundless. After an initial phase of dilemma, he realised the responsibilities and duties as a responsible resident of the UK, he having conferred with the right to reside here. The first step was to request his employer to register his employment with HM Revenue Service.

As he informed his parents back home; they were dire to see him. But it was not easy for Shan to travel to Bangladesh; he having previously denied of holding any Bangladeshi passport and since he had never submitted his passport to the Home Office therefore; all his time in the UK was considered illegal residence and he was required to build up five years legal residence before being qualified for naturalization as a British citizen.

Already; his parents elderly and frail, such a long wait was impossible, also the regular remittances from Shan and the construction of the new house with modern amenities on a new plot of land; at the highest point on the village to protect it from flood waters meant Shan wanted to see everything himself.

Desperate to travel; having discouraged by many that he will only loose the naturalization fees if he applies earlier; Shan ultimately contacted Ms Sen and immediately she assured that it will be done.

A year later; using her magic; Shan an illiterate nomadic farmer became a naturalized British citizen beating all odds; even fulfilling the English language criteria with assistance from Ms Sen, as the invigilator at the test centre directed Shan to tick the correct answers using her fingers. During the oath taking ceremony; Ms Sen accompanied him and by sheer bad luck Shan was selected randomly to read the oath loudly alone in front of the Registrar. Immediately Ms Sen intervened giving the excuse of a very bad sore throat and viral infection and the Registrar immediately declined the privilege to Shan; he himself being scared of catching the virus from Shan within close proximity; in the confined area. Ms Sen comfortably sat amongst the audience to witness the ceremony. Nobody actually heard or knew the oath Shan took, however; he was issued with a naturalization certificate; the gateway to apply for a British passport and to travel to Bangladesh.

When Ms Sen applied for naturalization on behalf of Shan just prior to the completion of one year since he was granted ILR, the application was straightway refused by the Home Office as Shan did not met any criteria under the Nationality Rules. But Ms Sen's perseverance and request after request giving arguments in favour of Shan paid off and Shan's application was approved at the Managerial level.

After receiving his British passport; Shan applied for a no visa stamp on his passport at the Bangladesh High Commission and was issued the same. But unknowingly this mistake on his part without consulting Ms Sen lead to wider implications on his life that was about to jeopardize everything; if Ms Sen had not been there.

Shan travelled to Bangladesh after more than fourteen years; he embarked at the Capital Dhaka and took the domestic flight to Sylhet. Shan's younger brother and his two nephews were at the Airport to pick him. Driving back home in the Toyota that his brother owned was a new experience. As the car ran in high speed through the four lane bitumen highway, Shan remembered; the awful journey to his maternal grandfather's house in the village; close to the Jamuna river by ox driven cart every year just before the monsoon as once the rains came in there was no time for entertainment but struggle for existence. Life would have remained standstill for his family too; if Shan had not taken up the challenge, like many other families living in the shanties or in remote villages.

The car went inside the big gates of a massive two storey building surrounded by high walls; Shan got out of the car, his parents and sister-in-law with her little daughter was standing. His parents instantly became emotional but Shan kept looking around the massive house, more like a mansion; mirror-like polished floors, exquisite choice of paint colours, breathtakingly spectacular interior and exterior design that match like twins. The outside lawn is trimmed and in an immaculate condition. It took him no time to understand that the pounds siphoned by him to his family has changed their lives and they in-fact are now used to a more comfortable life than his in the UK, where he had been living in the cramped staff accommodation above the restaurant with no basic amenities, it does not have a central heating system and no kitchen. Therefore; he is everyday forced to have the same meal chosen by Rois' elder brother-in-law, the Manager of the Restaurant.

Shan saw domestic maids, gardeners, a driver and a security guard, all on the pay roll of his family working 24/7 to enabling everyone to have a comfortable life. Shan was guided to his room by his sister-in-law, a young girl from Sylhet town, who has gone to college and studied up to BA first year, she is not the typical shy girl from the village, Shan had expected. Straightway without hesitation; she started asking questions about England and was very curious to know.

The long journey and jet- lag had made Shan tired and exhausted, he was dire to have a shower, eat and sleep; therefore he had to ask to be excused.

The next morning Shan woke up early and went out straight to have stroll in the area, in the new colony mostly occupied by new class of few economically affluent families whose any member has like him risked everything and made it to Europe or America. The mark of the dollar/ pound/ euro was visible everywhere, building massive houses as a show off not knowing the hardships who had paid for it all.

Nobody knew Shan in the area, and he had no intention to make new friends.

Slowly as he left past the pitched road and came down to village road still wet by the dew, he walked past the bamboo grove and could see the cluster of mud houses at a distance with smoke rising from the earthen oven set alight by the women to boil the rice grains, Shan has seen her mother doing the same at all times except during the floods. Little has changed in here except the local secondary school a pucca two storey building. Shan continued walking until he reached the banks of Jamuna waiting to be soaked in the colour of the rising sun. The new embankments though broken at few places were high and this has been a noticeable improvement that must have changed the lives of millions of the less fortunate dotted in villages along the bank of one of the fiercest river of the country.

The memories of growing up, in the village and the adolescence years, the stagnation, poverty, hunger all came back to him in a moment, the sight of the river, now calm and wide brought irresistible grief and he stood still. The mild air, the singing of birds, the rhythmic beats of the Palm tree leaves, the birds singing to greet the spring morning; the funeral pyre from the adjacent local burning area of dead bodies by the

Hindus suddenly brought back the feeling that little have changed and unknown to him, Shan kept walking following the bank of Jamuna, a river that made life miserable for him, is today the source of his mental solace around which nothing has moved with time, giving Shan the opportunity to identify himself and connect with his roots. He had no idea of the distance he had covered on foot and when the sun had come out in full glare and started heating up the world beneath, Shan came across a group of young and old women; bathing in the river, the young under the watchful eyes of the matriarchs to keep them safe from evil. Shan immediately took cover behind a huge Babla tree that has been there since time immemorial and Shan often took a nap, under the foliage during the afternoon at summer time while grazing the animals when temperature rose above 40 degree centigrade. As Shan could not but gazed at the bathing women, he being starved of native beauty in England for more than one and half decade. His eyes caught the sight of a young girl; wild fearful eyes, staying close to an elderly lady, she took a dip into the water and as she raised revealing herself, Shan saw her wasp-waisted figure, implying virginity and pureness and wet glossy skin all sparkling in the sunshine, she then sat on the bank and started rubbing soap trying her best to wade off the dirt, revealing all parts of her body, her bare back covered by her ebony-black hair and more often she raised her slender eyebrows and looked for unwanted onlookers. Her open breasts with brown tits all visible as she was busy caressing herself running her fingers all over her body, Shan was enjoying all her moves when suddenly she broke into a smile, revealing her beguiling, oyster-white teeth that jolted him like an electric current and Shan had instantly made up his mind that if he will marry a Bangladeshi girl, she will be the girl.

The long walk on empty stomach, the heat of the sun had made Shan tired and exhausted and he sat down on the newly constructed platform under the tree as if it had been built for the purpose; waiting for him all the time.

Shan sat there; as the group of women passed him, they were giggling and constantly chirping but his unexpected presence in such a desolate location caused a visible uproar amongst them and instantly they all went quiet; struggling to cover the bare parts of their body, started pulling clothes in all directions. A curious elderly lady came up to him enquiring and was more than satisfied knowing that Shan is from London and is visiting Bangladesh to get married, she immediately showed interest referring to the young women in the group from the neighbouring village. Shan politely asked the name of the village, the group disappeared behind the bamboo grove.

It was not that Shan had not seen a naked female body, he being a frequent visitor at C-DOZ Night Club, almost since the last ten years, every Tuesday with Dulal where intimate men and women were a common sight. Shan kept looking at the Jamuna, with the water raising the endless rhythmic waves with golden caps on them made it look proud, as if boasting to the sun of its immaculate beauty and fearsome power. He could distinctively see her sculpted figure, twine-thin, raising from the waters of Jamuna like a mermaid. Her waist was tapered and she had a burnished complexion. A pair of arched eyebrows looked down on sweeping eyelashes. Her delicate ears framed a button nose. A set of dazzling, angel-white teeth gleamed as she blew gently on her carmine-red fingernails towards him when he tried to touch her.

Shan returned home late; everyone was anxiously waiting for him in the courtyard with a bearded man sitting on the chair, he was introduced to Shan by his mother as 'Usman Chacha' the plumber and in his spare time he tends his goats. As Shan talked, he found out that he also 'arranges' marriages between two families and his mother has requested him to find a bride for Shan. Usman happily said he's arranged at least 100 of them, having known everybody around here and people trust him. His small shop; ten meters from the entrance of the village and so he knows who comes in with who and at what time and whether they're on drugs or are drunk. He said he likes to arrange marriages, even if it is a risk (people might blame him if things don't work out), and boasted that because of his noble work he will straight away go to heaven after death.

Marriage is a very important event in a person's life in South Asia and people marry young as dating is frowned upon by most people. Shan already in his mid-forties and still a bachelor was unusual. Weddings; typically last at least three days as there are several traditions that need to be observed both on the groom's and bride's side. Most marriages are arranged or at least partially arranged and for most South Asians it will be the first time the bride and groom will really get to know each other. Therefore, wedding is a big event involving immediate and extended families on both sides and marriages are not just about two people tying the knot but it is the coming together of two families. So hundreds of people are usually invited, fed and entertained with huge expenses incurred by both families.

To discourage Usman; in his efforts to find a bride for him, Shan expressed his desire not being ready for marriage. His parents went mute and Usman left with the warning and doubt that Shan might have been already married to an English woman in London.

After Usman's departure; Shan told his brother about the girl from next village, he has seen in the morning and his desire to get married to her. The same evening Shan's brother and mother went to the next village and managed to locate Zoya's house, with help and guidance from locals.

Zoya; aged 18 years was the only daughter of the sister of four brothers; Zoya's four maternal uncles, with strong political and criminal connections and her second uncle had been to prison charged with political murders a few times but each time walked out free in absence of proof.

Zoya's uncles were her guardian and nobody had seen her father once; since Zoya's mother returned home pregnant. Shan's brother had already made up the story that they have been guided by a friend to bring the proposal but it did not convince Zoya's guardians. They clearly expressed that they are looking for a young man, leaving Shan's mother with no other choice but to reduce Shan's age by 20 years and making him the youngest of the siblings.

Initially extremely reluctant; Zoya's uncles' ultimately gave their consent after Shan's promise that he will take Zoya with him to the UK as soon as possible. Given Shan's extremely tight schedule the marriage date was fixed the next week and everything was arranged in a rush.

Shan's mother insisted to fix the marriage date consulting the Bengali Calendar avoiding the inauspicious days that can destroy Shan's life, but unfortunately no suitable date can be found in the next week and Shan could not wait.

Despite; the date and month being inappropriate for the marriage; all the rituals were observed neatly on both houses starting the day before the marriage; exchange and smearing of turmeric paste on the bride and the groom, and their families, which is considered to be lucky as well as purifying and lightening the skin. There was song and dance during the ceremony.

On the actual day of the marriage, the signing of the contract or 'nikah' which sets how much the woman will receive in case of divorce or separation was done, but Shan's details were all wrong in the contract.

Shan had already spoken to a member of the local Council responsible for officially registering marriages to help him change the details and reissue the certificate in exchange for a hefty bribe, so that his wife can use it to travel to the UK, otherwise with the present details she stood no chance.

CHAPTER 28

On their wedding night Zoya was incredibly nervous, Shan tried to pick up a conversation about her likings, any previous sex experience and pregnancy plan but there was little response from her side. Frustrated by her unresponsiveness, Shan started kissing her lips and fondling her, nibbling her nipples and kissing all over her body, though extremely exhausted Shan managed to get a hard on and forced himself in, immediately afterwards he knocked out.

Early morning; the next day, the man from the Council came and delivered the Marriage Certificate with the correct details citing Shan's address in the UK as his home address, right age and no father's details. Shan was happy that he had managed everything so far efficiently.

Around 10 am in the morning; Zoya's uncles' accompanied by a group came into the house; forcing their entry into the courtyard shouting and screaming, abusing Shan, some threatening with direct action for his misdeed; initially neither Shan nor his family could predict the reason for their visit. Almost immediately they started hurling insulting words towards Shan for hiding his age and accusing him of being a bastard. When Shan's father wanted to know the reason, one of her uncle's thrashed the Marriage Certificate in front of Shan's father.

Badu Miah; who only knew to till the reclaimed lands on the banks of Jamuna, was still unable to find out the reason behind their anger. Zoya's second uncle came forward and explained everything to Badu Miah. Shan stood speechless, understanding the mood, it was impossible for him to defend or provide any explanation.

Shan ran upstairs to talk to Zoya before she misunderstands him. He tried to explain his situation and tell Zoya whatever he did was for her; so that she can join him immediately. Zoya just kept looking at him vaguely. Her uncles' downstairs demanded that she should immediately leave with them and started shouting her name. As Zoya was about to be stepped out of the room, Shan tried to stop her but in vain.

Zoya left with her uncles' who promised revenge and a huge compensation for the treachery and fraud committed by Shan, her uncle was informed by a disgruntled clerk who did not receive a fair share of the pie.

One of her uncle's boasted that he will get Shan arrested and he will languish in prison for the next 10 years for ruining the life of their only daughter. As the crowd left with area, gradually neighbours started coming in, enquiring about the ruckus, a day after the marriage and the bride leaving the house.

Shan's family did their best to cover up but could not satisfy their inquisitiveness, in the evening as rumour rose that soon the police will arrest Shan, he left the house, in the cover of the dark, his brother had already purchased a ticket from a travel agent in Sylhet city paying four times the cost, as his details had to be entered removing another passenger who had already purchased a ticket.

At Sylhet Airport; Shan exhibited symptoms of stress and anxiety, until he managed to check in and preceded towards immigration control .As Shan handed over his Red passport to the Bangladeshi official for stamp, he suddenly looked at the screen in his front and looked at Shan. After doing this a few times; he told Shan that he has no permission to enter the country. He asked Shan to wait in the side and left his desk with Shan's passport. It seemed like an unending moment, Shan was scared to death, he felt his legs stuck to the ground and going heavy. Ideas started racing through his mind about the consequences if he is not allowed to board the flight and Police arrests him. He was no longer prepared to live in hell having used to live in the heaven, Shan promised to himself that he will never return to Bangladesh the second time. Suddenly, a man was calling him from near the side toilet and he demanded money telling that the no visa stamp issued on his passport by the Bangladeshi authorities in the UK was inappropriate and for that reason he can be stopped leaving the country and prosecuted. Shan immediately offered to pay to get back his passport and started taking out all the pounds he had in his pocket and handed it to the man, who put the money in his pocket without counting and asked him to collect his passport from the counter. Shan speedily walked up to the desk and this time the man handed over his passport without a word. Shan literally ran towards the departure lounge.

In the long ten hour flight from Sylhet to London Heathrow, Shan could hardly understand what actually had happened to him in Bangladesh. He was confused, could not eat or sleep just repented his actions.

At Heathrow; Shan passed through the biometric scanner, he had no luggage and left the airport, as he walked out, he felt to be on the most peaceful place on earth, the warm May sunshine welcomed him, he somehow identified himself with the city and the feeling that it is his city and country, gave him enormous relief.

Shan took the Virgin train from Euston to Manchester, where rain welcomed him; he even enjoyed the drizzling as he walked from the train station towards the restaurant. Everybody was startled to see him back after a week and walking to the workplace.

By the time Shan reached 'Jalnupur', he was in tatters, Dulal took him aside and gave him the terrible news that Rois had a heart attack and is admitted to hospital. He also asked him to go to the accommodation and take rest. Shan was scared to do so; knowing that nothing but only work can make him overcome the trauma.

CHAPTER 29

The next four years; Shan only contacted his family, his father Badu Miah passed away soon, he could not recover from the humility the family had to undergo within the community. Shan's mother was indeed a brave lady who did not spare anybody dared to talk evil about her son.

His brother and sister-in-law had moved to Sylhet city, where there was more work and his brother owned a taxi base with few hundred taxis operating under him. Shan never missed Bangladesh, surprisingly; Zoya's family never brought any allegations against him involving the Police which was a relief.

His mother remained alone in the house supported by aides and one day to his surprise gave the message to Shan that he has a four year old son and Zoya's family had contacted her, sending a school application form for Shan to sign so that the child can be admitted to a boarding school, in Darjeeling, India.

Shan was taken aback; he requested his mother to forward the application form to him in the UK and it was from the school application form Shan found Zoya's address and wrote a brief letter; five years after they parted.

The initial letters were brief and upon Shan's request a few photographs of Zoya and her son was forwarded to him. Shan also started calling Zoya regularly and it was during these conversations he insisted that she and the child should join him in the UK.

But a delay of five years meant that a lot of water has flown down the Thames, and there had been significant change in policy and outlook by the successive Government in the UK, determined to cap immigration, implementing strict laws and conditions that meant it was the beginning of a challenge that Shan was due to take.

Since his return to the UK after a disastrous marriage attempt; Shan lived within himself, he worked seven days a week and interacted little with others. He never once visited the Club at Oxford Road, ignoring repeated requests from Dulal where before; they were regular visitors; on Tuesdays. It is not that Shan didn't try to totally wipe out Zoya from his memory but could not do so; in his personal life he had to deal with challenging perceptions of isolation, boredom and frustration. On the other hand, while at work; he became extremely creative and perfect; his passion for food and fusion between different tastes across borders experimented for the first time, created ripples making him the unchallenging winner of ' the best curry chef' award every year. As if; Shan's skills as 'a chef' were getting refined with time and customers were crazy about his dishes. On weekends; the Restaurant remained open till 2.00am in the morning. While other businesses were closing down, Rois and Shan kept afloat.

Four years after their separation, upon Zoya's approval and eagerness to come to the UK with Raza, Shan again contacted Ms Sen to help him to bring his wife and child. After; hearing the whole episode; Ms Sen was sceptical about the paternity of Raza and she knew that given the date of marriage and Shan's return to the UK, immediately afterwards, whether the British High Commission will accept the paternity of Raza without a DNA analysis. She however came up with the brilliant idea to apply for his wife first and once his wife is granted entry clearance, sort out Raza's case and apply for a British passport for him; giving reference to the mother's application and using the new British passport issued to Shan in lieu of a lost passport that will help him erase all dates. Meanwhile;

Zoya was instructed to pursue an English language course, to sit for a specific test otherwise she will be unable to submit her application.

Shan prepared all the paperwork in the UK and forwarded the same to Zoya; she was elated upon receiving them. Zoya; the only daughter of her maternal family; no longer enjoyed the status co she had within the family before. Her aunties were zealous and did not spare any opportunity to rebuke her. Her mother was too depressed to look after Raza and she only had the support of her grandmother and great grandmother; the two matriarch's who were struggling to bring up her son.

Zoya was a reckless and rebellious eighteen year old when her marriage failed. Two months later; she was found pregnant, however; the doctor checked and declined to do an abortion leaving her with no choice but to continue with it.

Her son; Raza was born seven months after her marriage; despite the complications during delivery; he was a healthy baby but Zoya had little interest in him. The child was looked after by his great grandmother and great great grandmother whilst Zoya continued with her daily routine; she restarted her college so that she can complete her studies and get a job to have a respected life afterwards. The next three years passed smoothly but as Raza completed his fourth birthday, her uncles' decided that he should be sent to a boarding school in Darjeeling, India to keep him permanently out of his mother's life so that Zoya can remarry and resettle.

Though initially Zoya had some objections but thinking it would be best for the child and she will be independent, she agreed. While in the process of applying to the school a year ahead of the academic session, her uncle sent the application form by post to Shan's house so that it can be forwarded to him in the UK and returned in time. But things changed permanently for Zoya and Raza once Shan was contacted.

Zoya; however had to deal with one of her uncle who had some issues regarding what was going on and insisted that she should refuse Shan's proposal instead get a divorce and remarry. Nonetheless; Zoya was dire to see the unseen and she was not willing to listen. Her regular conversations with Shan that started initially very formal remained so but became more regular and frequent. As Shan was preparing the documents and the application through a solicitor; the frequency and duration of contact enhanced.

Under the latest evolution of the Immigration Rules aimed to lower migration from non EU countries and stop force marriages in South Asian countries Zoya had to qualify under various criteria of the rules covering all aspects; starting from her meeting to marriage, the duration of cohabitation till the time her husband left for UK, contact thereafter, whether she met the English language skills and for her husband to have an income equivalent to a certain amount; at a rate much higher than the calculations of the benefits agency and proof of adequate accommodation.

Given Shan's particular history and the length of the marriage it was important to draft the application meticulously covering all the different criteria and avoiding any complications.

Therefore; it was put forward that Zoya first met her husband in Sylhet, Bangladesh at a friend's house while he was on holiday in Bangladesh and they liked each other. Following a marriage proposal by Shan; the marriage was arranged by Zoya's mother; with help from her uncles and they got married; a week later in a ceremony attended by friends and relatives and the marriage was registered as per Bangladesh Marriage Act.

Following the marriage, it was unfortunate that Shan had to rush back to the UK, following an emergency as his friend and business partner; Rois suffered a heart attack which was 100% true, supported by documentary evidence, a letter from Rois detailing all the support and help he had from Shan during that time, to look after his business affairs that ultimately prompted him to make the decision to make him a shareholder at the business. Given Rois' stature as the ex-Lord Mayor of Manchester, his testimony could not have been negated and it was true; in the real sense.

Zoya stressed that though Shan had to leave in a hurry but they remained in regular contact over the phone, providing old phone cards used by Shan's work colleagues.

The failure on the part of Shan to visit his wife in Bangladesh at any time during the last almost five years was put on Shan's busy work schedule due to shortage of Curry Chef's in the UK. A bulk of greetings cards with envelopes covering the entire period, all with fake stamps were included and the marriage photographs and video recording of the entire marriage ceremony was incorporated. Zoya's continuing education after marriage was given an excuse too. Zoya maintained that she will live with her mother until the time she joins her husband in the UK. It was stressed upon that Zoya fulfils the relationship requirements subjected to specific paragraph of the new immigration rules.

Zoya had already successfully passed City & Guilds International Speaking and Listening; IESOL Diploma at Preliminary A1 level from the College in Sylhet town and was awarded certificates for that. Therefore; she truly met the English language requirement that required passing an English language test in speaking and listening at a minimum of level A1 of the Common European Framework of Reference for Languages with a provider approved by the UK Border Agency.

In regard to Shan's settled status in the UK, minimum information was divulged only providing the dates he was granted settlement and naturalized as a British citizen.

Though Shan had enough savings in his bank account, equivalent to fifty thousand pounds and more; he having worked hard all his life in the UK and rest of the money three times the amount being siphoned to his family in Bangladesh but it was almost impossible for him to proof the source of his earnings due to the scrupulousness of his employer and business partner; Rois who never showed him working full time to avoid tax. Also; despite Shan being a share holder at the company and receiving dividends regularly, he had no paperwork.

Shan was required to show a gross annual income nearing nineteen thousand pounds per annum; to call his wife to the UK. But Rois' tax fraud meant that he could only show an income less than ten thousand pounds from the employment. In reality; Shan was working forty five hours and earning an amount equivalent to £500 in cash every week.

So; even the money was deposited in his bank account; Shan had no evidence to back it up. Therefore; it was maintained that due to the financial crunch and loss of business; Shan was only working part-time; 20 hours a week that raised an income close to nine thousand five hundred pounds, substantiated by proof; his wage slips and annual tax return form. It was then put forward that Shan is a shareholder at the company holding 25 ordinary shares of the total shares in issue of which there are 100 ordinary shares. He received Gross Dividend amounting to £9444 in the last financial year which was true but he did not have the relevant paperwork except a letter from the Accountants of the business confirming his gross annual income from salary and dividends.

Zoya maintained that her husband's total income from employment and dividends for the last financial year exceeded the qualifying amount, close to nineteen thousand and therefore she can be maintained and accommodated in the UK without any recourse to public funds.

Despite having such large savings in various bank accounts; Shan never bought any property or tried to take out a mortgage. He being content with living in the free cramped shared Restaurant accommodation provided by Rois.

But to bring his wife; Shan had to provide a tenancy agreement, so he rented one of the properties owned by Rois as a joint tenant. The property consisted of 3 bedrooms, and he had to employ the local council inspector to certify that there is ample accommodation for Zoya at the property and it was free from hazards and fit for human habitation as defined by the relevant Housing Act in the UK.

Zoya's application also raised human rights grounds that is meant to protect the family life involving husband and wife and their right to live together in a unit without any interference by a public authority unless it is necessary to do so; in the interests of national security, public safety or the economic well being of the country, for the prevention of disorder or crime, for the protection of health or morals, or for the protection of the rights and freedoms of others.

Zoya stressed that her application is a genuine one and she should therefore be allowed to join her husband.

Despite Bangladesh's liberalized visa regime for United Kingdom citizens and people from other developed and developing countries, to attract international tourists. Zoya knew that crossing the hurdle will not be easy and she always had a lingering tension - will she get the visa or not? All sorts of worries, some more rational than others, plagued her mind.

She was not satisfied with the proofs provided by Shan in regard to his earning except his bank balance which was big enough. She wandered; will some mean-spirited visa officer who had a bad breakfast that morning or a fight with the spouse the night before take it all out on her application? Whether embassies have rejection targets?

Zoya's visa was refused after almost three months as the Entry Clearance Officer (ECO) did not accept the earnings of Shan, on grounds that not enough proof has been provided concerning his shareholding in the company, which the ECO considered to be self employment and maintained that Shan has not registered his self employment with the Tax Office, leaving Zoya with no other option but to put up a legal challenge.

Zoya challenged the decision maintaining that the ECO having completely overlooked the fact that her husband is employed with Jalnupur Restaurant Ltd and is also a shareholder in the Limited Company; enclosing a letter from Greenhare Chartered Tax Advisers & Accountants; the Tax Advisers for Rois; confirming that Limited Companies do not have self employed personnel; only Directors and Shareholders. Therefore there is no obligation on Shan to be registered with HMRC. The letter also confirmed that Shan is a shareholder of Jalnupur Restaurant Ltd- details of which can be found on the Annual Return that was forwarded to the Companies House; with the following information that Shan holds 25 ordinary shares of the total shares in issue of which there are 100 ordinary shares. He received Gross Dividend amounting to nine thousand four hundred and forty four pounds in the last financial year. The claim was substantiated by proof; Tax Vouchers indicating Shan receiving the same amount as dividend for the last financial year ending. The Report of the Director and the Unaudited Financial Statements for the previous Year of the business showing the net profit and the Dividends amounting to £34000 and Shan received £8500 of it (holding 25 ordinary shares) + £944(Tax Credit) amounting to £9444.The Company Tax Return Form CT600 (2008) Version 2 established the tax paid by the Company to HM Revenue & Customs.

Zoya also gave reference to the raised wages of Shan due to increase in working hours and rate and stressed that her husband's total earnings from employment and as a shareholder in the business exceeds £18,600 as evident from the documents therefore she requested the ECO to kindly review her application.

After waiting for more than a year; Zoya's case came to the Court. Shan left no stone unturned; he hired one of the best Immigration barristers, accompanied by Rois and the Accountant's representative; he went to the Court and without the support of an interpreter; assuming that the majority of the questioning related to his employment had to be answered by Rois and the Accountant.

While at the hearing; the Judge, who had met Rois on several occasions during his tenure as the Lord Mayor of Manchester, accepted every word of his and without any clarification from the Accountants and not bothering Shan, within less than ten minutes, he decided to allow Zoya's appeal on her favour recommending a fee refund by the Home Office.

Shan pump his fists in the air and praise the lord, he could not wait but to give the good news to Zoya, thousands of miles away; the anxiety associated with the wait had already horribly affected her, as the delay was jeopardising Raza's education.

It was preparation time and time for Shan to travel back to his homeland the second time, to bring his family. Immediately; he lost his passport and made a police report, to bury his precarious travel history that would have seriously affected any application for a British passport for Raza; his father having left Bangladesh the very next day after his marriage.

Only with two weeks holidays; in hand Shan travelled to Bangladesh with the enormous challenge to take out the British passport for his son, so that he could travel with his mother.

After reaching Bangladesh; travelling on his new passport, Shan came to know that the British High Commission in Bangladesh has closed down and all applications submitted through an agent are processed in neighbouring India; something that gave him enormous relief, the British passport application form completed by an agent was forwarded to the Diplomatic Post in India, without any interview. Shan's self proclamation and his name on the birth certificate was enough. Shan could not wait for the outcome as he had to return to the UK.

Raza's British passport was picked up by his mother and within three months of the Judge's decision, the embassy through the local agent in Sylhet asked for Zoya's passports and returned the same after a week with the shiny visa stamp with her photo on it. After receiving the visa; Zoya; grumbled for the unnecessary long wait she had to undergo when often she felt guilty and like a fool for wanting to set foot in another country.

Nevertheless, the drama she considered part of the build-up to her trip abroad, unknowing of the consequences, she was overwhelmed with joy and immediately started packing her bags, taking bits of everything she was advised to take.

Zoya and Raza boarded the flight from Sylhet and after a long tiring journey arrived at Heathrow. Raza clung to his mother; they crossed all the hurdles and ultimately came out with their luggage.

Shan was waiting for them in the waiting lounge, he having travelled to Heathrow a day earlier and already hired a taxi to bring his family to Manchester.

The three and half hour journey to Manchester was tiring for Zoya; but Raza remained un- beat until the break at Birmingham, but dozed off after that.

CHAPTER 30

Shan had for the first time in his life left the restaurant accommodation and had to make independent arrangement for his family. He having taken on rent a two bedroom house owned by Rois', situated in the suburbs of Oldham with the spectacular views of the Pennines at a distance; the hills and the meadows with serpentine roads on them.

Raza was admitted to the local Primary school and with no Asian family in the vicinity meant that Zoya's spoken English skills came into test almost immediately. Shan's long working hours and travelling to Manchester 7 days week meant, he had little time for his family. On weekdays; when Shan was dropped home by Dulal at midnight, Zoya and Raza were fast asleep. On weekends; it was worse; Shan sometime came home early in the morning. Whatever interaction Zoya had with Shan was during daytime from 10.00 to 11.00 am in the morning and from 3.00pm to 5.00pm, in the afternoon. However; every night the sound of the door wake her up before she slipped into deep sleep as Shan locked the door.

Zoya had no alternative but to manage everything on her own, she dropped and picked Raza from school, pretty close from home. Gradually, she started visiting the corner shop to buy anything essential. Soon; she settled into her routine, practically managing the house singlehanded and her outgoing nature meant, she was not finding it hard. The cold winter initially prohibited her, whenever; she was free she stood in the upstairs bedroom window, watching neighbours walking the dogs to the nearby mores. The serpentine road clinging to the hillside hazed by hill fog was empty most of the time, as drivers from Manchester avoided the road during the winter months.

One evening after putting Raza to bed, when cleaning the pots, Zoya suddenly noticed small white flakes falling from the sky, she couldn't but resist not opening the back door to feel it. She stepped outside in the backyard, stretched her arms and widely opened her mouth to catch them. Instantly her mind was joyful and she went round and round, in the snow, not feeling cold. After; a while she came in and run upstairs to see the view from the bedroom window stretched far out, what she witnessed was magical, white flakes in millions and trillions silently coming down, very different from the gloomy damp weather and loneliness she battled every day. Zoya could not move, she wanted to see the end of it, gradually the intensity and frequency of the snow increased curtailing her visibility and everything was turning white.

Zoya saw one or two passerby's passed leaving footprints on the snow and suddenly everything on the street looked bright and spotless. She stood watching the snow for countless time; thinking about the sheep she had seen in the open fields above the road and the deer herd in the nearby country park, how they are coping with the weather in the open, until the mobile phone rang breaking the silence. It was Shan, phoning her at midnight to say that heavy snowfall and closing down of the connecting main road meant; he will have to stay at the restaurant accommodation. He advised Zoya to put the latch in the main door before going to sleep.

But Zoya couldn't sleep that night, for the first time in her life; she had the opportunity to witness snowing; something she had heard in the village happens in London. It was not until early morning Zoya dozed off, waking up to the sound of the alarm clock. She jumped out of bed and ran to the window, removing the curtain she called Raza, who hearing his mother's cry, came out of bed reluctantly rubbing his eyes, only to shatter in astonishment, seeing everything covered in a thick white blanket.

Zoya made Raza ready for school and left home, the snow was sill soft, their feet dunging into it and had to put extra effort to lift it up. There was almost a 6-8 inches of snow, what normally took 8 minutes every day, took more than 15 minutes to reach, walking past the small hill side, Zoya saw parents with their children carrying plastic boards and going up the hill, it was a festive and fair atmosphere, many of the children's were from Raza's school. Upon reaching the school gate, Zoya saw a handwritten notice indicating the closure of the school for the day due to child safety reasons, she kept wondering what safety would have compromised for the children at school. So; Zoya and Raza started the return journey back home when reaching the hill-side, Raza broke free his hand and started running up the hill waving towards a boy. Zoya had to follow him. It was Raza's friend Alfee, they started throwing snow balls as Zoya stood and watched them, she also had the deep urge to join in the game but resisted. Standing in one foot deep snow made her feel cold but seeing Raza enjoying with his friend, she was ready to withstand any difficulties.

In the meantime; Alfee's mum tried to engage in a conversation with Zoya; she could hardly understood anything nodding and smiling in response.

After; more than an hour's play, Zoya and Raza returned home, Shan called to say that he will return home in the afternoon and will stay home until tomorrow, the first time Zoya saw him taking leave from work.

Shan's message meant that Zoya started cooking, she made all the preparations and the food was ready, before Shan arrived with Dulal around 2pm.There was more snowing and bad weather leading to Dulal staying until evening.

After a sumptuous meal, Dulal, Shan and Zoya sat down with tea and she told them about the incident with Alfee's mother, her inability to understand the English with a particular accent. Dulal insisted that she must be admitted to the local college that will keep her occupied and help her enormously with spoken English.

Since there was no chance for Shan to pass the driving test theory, Dulal suggested that Zoya should learn driving and make preparations for the theory test that will enable them to be independent and travel to Oldham and mingle with the Bangladeshi community.

The snow stooped that evening and under clear skies, in the full moon, the snow which had turned to ice, shined in the moonlight, everything wrapped in a white blanket, there was purity everywhere.

After Raza had gone to bed, Shan grabbed Zoya and pulled her close to him, he had his tongue inside her mouth, hers in him. It was so sweet! After two minutes or so; Zoya laid her body on him and he could feel her breast on his chest. Shan grabbed her butt and squeezed it. She moved her breast right in front of his face. Shan started to lick her chest and moved his hands slowly up her back. He grabbed her breasts and played with them in his hands. She started to breath heavier. Shan began to play with her tits and tease her clit through her pajamas. Zoya then unzipped Shan's pants and pull out his now very hard cock. Without saying a word she immediately put it in her mouth and started licking and sucking every inch of it! She licked all around the head of it because she knew how that drives him wild! Shan had to stop her because he was about to lose it. Shan pulled her up and have her sit on him. As he entered her it felt like a warm paradise wrapped around his cock. He slid into her without any problem because of her pussy was so wet and aching for his cock. She began to rock back and forth and riding him like a bucking bull, she then started to bounce up and down and grabbing her tits in extreme pleasure. Shan then took both breasts in his hands and began to suck both of her nipples as she still rode him.

Later; he took her and laid her down on the bed on her back and entered her again. Shan was in complete ecstasy looking at his wife laying there; enjoying all the pleasure she was getting. He loved to watch her tits bounce while he was trying to give her every inch he got. He could then feel her pussy start to tighten up around his cock and her juices began to come out around his, her moans began to get louder. Just about that time; Shan's mobile phone started ringing, it was Dulal, Shan came instantly, spoiling everything for Zoya who was in the middle of her orgasm. As Shan walked out of the room with his phone, Zoya felt dejected, her mind was filled with only one question; what was so important in the phone call that Shan had to answer immediately. Shan continued with his conversation in a low voice downstairs, by the time he came back Zoya was fast asleep.

CHAPTER 31

The next day; Raza's school opened and Zoya found it difficult to walk in the slippery hard snow, what began as a magical experience soon started fading and she began hating the solid slippery ice that severely impacted on her activities.

Dulal came in the morning braving the slippery roads to pick Shan but said he will not be coming in the afternoon break and will only return home at night. The next few days; with bitter cold winds; the snow kept its grip. Then at last; it rained and washed away every bit of the white staff except on the top of hills; at a distance.

Luckily there was no more snowing for the rest of the winter, one Sunday morning in March when Zoya put on the TV for Raza, she noticed the time has jumped by one hour, initially she thought; something wrong with the television. When Shan woke up, he confirmed that the time has gone forward by one hour on Saturday midnight. Something; beyond Zoya's understanding; of how the time can change by human intervention.

Though; Zoya was content with Raza's educational progress, his school was not, following concerns raised by his class teacher, about his limited speech and communication difficulties, for no other reason but his upbringing in Bangladesh until his arrival into the UK. Raza was put in the Special Education Needs Register at school. His school demanded funding from the local Council to provide one to one assistance to Raza in the classroom. The result was Raza was bombarded with a long list of appointments with various agencies involving the Local Hospital, Education Department and Social Services. The involvement of multi-agencies made Zoya extremely busy to keep up with the appointments as Raza's other parent was not available to attend the appointments due to his busy work schedule.

After repeated consultations with Consultant Pediatrician, Consultant Child Psychologist from the Child & Adolescent Mental Health Services (CAMHS), Educational Psychologist appointed by the Local Council under the guidance of a Social Worker for more than six months, Raza was identified as a vulnerable child with anxiety symptoms, consequently he was offered a highly personalized curriculum. Raza initially struggled to settle in school and was unable to develop friendships; staff at his school watched and guarded him constantly to provide the safety net, to keep him safe from the unruly children at playground.

Gradually; Zoya realised that the main problem with her son is rooted in his skin colour, the only Asian boy in his entire school and his struggle to assimilate; due to inhibitions not entirely due to his fault.

Zoya's first year in the UK passed unnoticed, despite the struggle, worries by his mother, Raza started Year 2 and before Zoya could contemplate the time passed unnoticed, the time again moved backward and the short winter days were back again. It started snowing severely from early November and the unimaginable hardships it brought for Zoya. To battle in the snow, attending her college to pass the English Language test, the final hurdle prior to her application for settlement, taking Raza to various appointments forced by his school to continue with the funding they received from the Local educational authority. Practicing her driving theory at home and slippery roads meant she had to stop her practical driving lessons. Zoya started to hate the snow; she no longer filled thrilled by it.

As it took long enough for Zoya to travel to Oldham city centre and visiting the hospital and local authority assessment centre; she regularly insisted that they should move house to nearby Oldham with a large Bangladeshi population to enable Raza to have a better life. Shan kept postponing the idea, in the pretext that Dulal is unable to find a suitable rented accommodation there.

Zoya's routine started every morning at 7.00 am, she left the house with Raza at 8.30 am dropped him at school and straightway went to college. Zoya having joined further Maths and English courses to enhance her skills, she finished classes at 2.30pm and on the way back home picked Raza from school.

Majority of the days when returning home, she found Dulal at the house and they both left for work at around 5.00pm.There was hardly any communication between Zoya and Shan and the damage that happened during this inception stage of the relationship never got the chance to repair, Zoya at times blamed herself for Shan's apathy towards her and the child.

Otherwise; Shan was an excellent husband, he worked hard seven days a week, he was a shareholder in the business, never asked Zoya about her spending but he was never there to be a part in the decision making process whenever such a need arise.

However; Zoya found her time at the college really exciting, particularly in the English class where her teacher was an Indian lady from Malaysia and the students were from various countries. Ms Lily, always used video clips; bringing the outside and practical applications of the English language inside the classroom that helped the students immensely. She also used simple worksheets and gave regular tasks to complete at home. Zoya at times struggled with her work at home but whenever she had a problem, she called Freddy, the strong build, Polish man from her class, a great admirer of her Briyani rice (rice cooked with meat). Zoya; took some time at college to come out of her cocoon, she was hesitant and reluctant, being new in the country. Seeing a white man learning English was a matter of great surprise. Gradually; she started participating in the class and took part in the 'Unity in Diversity' campaign, dressed in sari, she brought cooked spicy rice for her class-mates.

Freedy had never tasted such food but fell for the hot spicy rice, since that day they became good friends. Zoya showed him photos of Raza and Freedy, photographs of his son in Poland living with his maternal grandmother. Freedy met Alena, at a Christmas fair in Poznan when they both were only 15.The relationship continued for 5 years and Alena gave birth to a child from the relationship but soon after Edmund's birth, Alena moved to Warsaw with a rich businessman leaving Edmund with her mother. Freedy had very little work at Poznan, so he decided to move to the UK as an EU migrant.

Arriving in London by a bus was the experience of a life time. With no money, no hotel booking, he just arrived in the commercial capital of the world equipped with a backpack and a sleeping bag. The first few nights were spent in the park adjacent to Aldwich tube station, when unable to register himself with the Department of Social Services to get a National Insurance number; a must requirement to enable him to access job seekers allowance and training prior to entering the job market, following advice from a black Portuguese national who was also unable to register himself due to long queues at the Social security office, with new arrivals from the European Union queuing up since early morning and the office only providing limited number of tickets, enabling only few applicants to go inside the office and see a work adviser, Freedy decided to travel out of London.

He accompanied by Adebolaje; the Portuguese man, originally from Nigeria took the Mega bus to Manchester from Victoria Bus Station. After; almost six hours journey they reached Manchester. It was raining and Adebolaje told him that he had got the address of a Church where they will be able to find accommodation for few days before everything is sorted out. With no speaking ability in English and very limited understanding of the language Freedy relied on Adebolaje entirely. They managed to reach the Church in Clayton, in the south of Manchester. Father; Patrick was happy to provide accommodation to the two young men as Adebolaje took out a folded piece of paper from his wallet and handed it over to him.

He took them to upstairs from a side entrance and opened a room for them. It was a dormitory with six single steel bunk beds and there was a bathroom at the end of the corridor. Father Patrick carefully took the keys out of the key chain and handed it over to Adebolaje.

This was after almost five days Freedy had the opportunity to sleep on a bed, since he had left Poland. He dreamt of his child playing hide and seek with him in the park and suddenly lost in the traffic. As he was losing his breath, running amidst the double deck buses and black cabs looking for Edmund, shouting his name, he wake up sweating. Freedy had made up his mind that he will anyhow register with the department of Social Security and try to move things as fast as he could and sent money for Edmund in Poland.

The next morning; Freedy and Adebolaje left the Church, it was still drizzling. They took the bus to town and by the time they managed to locate the Social Security Office, there was a big rush of Romanians and in charge of the line was rough looking men charging one pound from everyone who stood there.

Before Freedy could realise, Adebolaje paid them two pounds but their turn never came. The next morning Freedy and Adebolaje returned to the office taking the first bus at 5 am. They were the first in the door. By 8 am, there were around 100 people and suddenly fight broke out started by one of the boys who were managing the line. One of the men took out a knife, and everyone ran, including Freedy and Adebolaje. After 10 minutes when the situation came under control, it was the Romanians who were in in-charge of the queue, Freedy and Adebolaje had lost their position in the line. They understood; it was useless to stand in the queue and pay money to the Romanians. It became outside the apprehension of these men, of how things work in the UK as Freedy and Adebolaje found them in a despicable situation. With few coins left; Freedy went to the local supermarket and bought a loaf. They returned to the Church and shared the bread between themselves with free tea obtained at the Church. That afternoon; Father Patrick called them, to say that delegates from Ireland are coming to stay that evening and despite his best intentions he cannot accommodate them anymore.

When Freedy and Adebolaje left the Church that evening, it was still raining; the rain hasn't stopped since they had arrived into the city more than 56 hours before. With nowhere to spend the night; they decided to go to the city centre and spent night somewhere under a shelter. The strong westerly winds meant there was a chill in the air. Freedy and Adebolaje decided to spend the night under the balcony of the opera house; opposite the Hilton Hotel. With no daytime preparation, no cardboards to spread and one sleeping bag they struggled to keep warm. Occasionally; there was the black cab bringing guests to the hotel. Early; in the morning, a guard from the Opera House came out to give them warning that they are not allowed to be there. However; the guard from Nigerian origin spoke to Adebolaje in Yoruba and through him they learnt about the City of Oldham where they will be able to register with the Social Services the same day.

Instead of queuing up in front of the Manchester office, Freddy and Adebolaje took the lift from Mr. Folarin who dropped them in front of the Job Centre at Oldham Town Centre well before 9 am. There was nobody in the queue and when the Office opened they stepped inside. Freedy was assessed by a Bangladeshi caseworker who seeing his condition immediately put him into the hostel and asked him to return the next day.

The registration went smoothly; Freedy was told to wait for a few days until the time he receives his National Insurance Number. In the meantime; he was advised to open a bank account and provide the details to his caseworker to enable him to forward a crisis loan. He was flag shipped to the College to learn English.

Learning English was fun; with regular job seekers allowance deposited in his account, he accumulated enough money to visit Poland and bring his son to the UK for registration to enable him to obtain child benefit for Edmund.

Edmund's maternal grandmother was reluctant to allow him to travel with his dad but the lust of regular money for Edmund that will give him the best opportunities crave in and she gave permission.

Freedy brought Edmund to UK by bus, straightway took him to the Social Security Office for registration and next day he took him back to Poland. Freedy had no choice; the one night Edmund was with him, he could not sleep at the hostel and had to stay at the hotel.

Gradually; Freedy developed relationship with all his classmates, including Zoya, whose son was the same age of Edmund. Freedy was hugely relieved after he started receiving the weekly child benefit for Edmund which he sent to Poland on a monthly basis.

It was during Zoya's participation in the 'Unity in Diversity' program that she actually became friends with all her classmates who univocally advocated her beauty and her food, recommending her as the best chef; and creating such a fusion dish; combining rice with meat and potatoes.

After; the program everybody started interacting with Zoya and gradually she became a part of the class; but she became good friends with Freedy.

Both learning English; meant talking to each other helped both of them to enhance their speaking and listening skills; a mandatory requirement for Zoya before she is granted settlement in the UK. For Freedy it was important because without understanding the language, his job prospects were nil.

Apart from her assignments and lessons at class, every evening Zoya listened to BBC news as per the instructions of her tutor, in the first weeks Zoya hardly understood what was being said except the prepositions, nouns, pronouns, verbs, adverbs, adjectives separately. Her efforts to follow what was being said gradually yielded result and she started understanding. Zoya never gave up the habit in the rest of her life; watching the news for an hour whenever she returned home.

Freedy wanted to meet Raza; one afternoon in the summer when Shan phoned to say he is busy shopping with Dulal and will not return home, Zoya called Freedy over. Raza and Freedy almost bonded immediately; they went out for a walk in the nearby hills.

Henceforth; whenever Shan did not return Zoya called over Freedy. They spent the entire day together and Freedy returned home after dinner.

Together they even attended the school fair at Raza's school; setting up a small shop and sold items £1 each, selling Raza's cloths, toys and crockery, making 35-40 pounds from the sale. Freedy refused any share allowing Zoya to keep the entire profit. The shop was a big fun and Zoya and Raza enjoyed selling items to white people. Zoya did not even bother to sell those items that were still usable.

Gradually; it became a routine that Freedy started coming every afternoon after college and spent the evening with Zoya and Raza. Before; Zoya could apprehend; she was about to complete her courses at the college. After the examination, in the end of June, the college closed down for summer break. Soon after Raza's school also closed down for six weeks holidays.

The day; she sat for the examination; Zoya returned home with a heavy heart, confused about how to spent the entire day alone. In the next few days; she phoned Freedy regularly and he came over in the afternoon.

In July; the results came out both Zoya and Freedy passed the ESOL Level 3 course in English. Shan was relieved that at least Zoya will be able to apply for settlement immediately. As soon as Freedy passed the English course; the Department of Work insisted that he should now find employment and exercise his treaty rights in the UK. Freedy tried hard to find a job in Oldham but could not, forcing him to apply for Jobs elsewhere. At last he was hired by a removal company in London. Freedy moved to London just before Christmas and over the months gradually lost contact with Zoya.

CHAPTER 32

Zoya started concentrating on her driving lessons and she started preparing for the theory test. Soon; it was time for her to apply for settlement. Dulal took her to the nearby Law Centre where she was handed over a sixty page form for completion and submission to the Home Office.

It took consisted efforts by Zoya, Dulal and Shan to complete the form and arrange the documents. Two weeks before the expiry of her visa; Zoya posted her application to the Home Office enclosing her passport, Shan's passport and Raza's passport and a long list of documents. Though the Home Office was quick to acknowledge the application and took the application processing fees from Shan's account but thereafter; the waiting game begun. Months passed and Zoya kept waiting, hoping that her passport will come any day with the settlement sticker on it and a year later she will have her red passport.

Every morning Zoya ran to the front door to pick up the post, she almost became aware of the timing the postman came.

Then suddenly; after five months; in May, one Saturday morning the doorbell rang, Zoya run for it and received a big packet from the postman.

She opened the packet with extreme excitement and found all the documents and Shan and Raza's passport in it. As she searched frantically amidst the bundle, she noticed a refusal letter within it.

Zoya couldn't read the letter and tears gushed down her cheeks; thinking that everything is over and she will have to return to Bangladesh, she lost all hope. Shan immediately called Dulal and tried to contact Ms Sen.

When Dulal came and read the refusal letter; it was understood that Home Office refused Zoya's application because she had used the wrong version of the application form for such type of applications. Home Office retained Zoya's passport citing that she should submit a new application.

Those two days were the longest days of Zoya's life, the only 2 page letter from Home Office made everything upside down. She lost her appetite and sleep, she became irritant and her grief and fear vented out through unprovoked outbursts towards Raza when Shan was absent from home.

Shan requested Dulal to take them to Ms Sen the following Monday, after a long wait their turn came, they handed over the papers to her and Zoya signed a new application form, Shan paid the fees and was assured that she will take care of the rest.

Ms Sen had no other alternative but to submit a new application form on Zoya's behalf to the Home Office, she also requested the Home Office to return the application fee for the first application.

Since submitting the initial application in the month of January Zoya's life was at halt, in absence of a passport she couldn't enroll at the college, nor complete her driving. Gradually; spending all the time alone at home Zoya was becoming paranoid, she started hearing voices, suffered from depression and anxiety, the frustration was at times so intense that she contemplated suicide. At times; she blamed Shan for not making the initial application through Ms Sen, Shan and Dulal's closeness and Shan following his advice word to word all the time and Dulal's involvement in all family matters became clearer to her; she started hating him.

Whenever; she felt claustrophobic inside; she went out for a walk in the nearby hills where the hissing of the air annoyed her. She started missing her village, the memories of her childhood, her growing up and the particular incident of rape; started coming back frequently. She and Mita as they entered the narrow lane behind the post office to make the short-cut to catch a cycle van to go home, being already late that afternoon; having skipped class and went to see a Hindi movie at the Regent Cinema. Suddenly; from behind the banyan tree four figures appeared and before Zoya and Mita could make a sound, they were taken inside a white van. The struggle for freedom was vicious and she remembers every bit of it as she started kicking and punching the men, biting and pushing them hard. Last thing she remembers was something hitting her head.

Zoya woke up in the arm of a tough well build man and she was bare, the man was stroking her breasts hard. Trapped between his heavy legs Zoya couldn't move and he said today was payback day for her dad, for still not leaving the country despite numerous warnings. The country that was born to be a holy land cannot tolerate infidels and the land does not belong to them. Zoya couldn't understand a word he was saying. He held her hand, took off her panties, and then raped her, he was violent, he was rough, he called her names, he insulted her, he even spit on her and all through he held a knife to her neck, it felt like an eternity, eventually he stopped, zipped up his pants and left the room. Zoya stood dazed and confused, what had just happened, she thought she was dreaming, suddenly she felt a bit damp and discovered herself soaked, and she was in so much pain despite that she gathered strength, put on her cloths and came out of the room to find her friend; Mita; who couldn't be found. Nobody stopped her and she slowly walked out of the house. It was late evening and the streetlights seemed lightless everything was dark and grey except the howling of the barn owl. She kept walking aimlessly, not aware of her exact location. Seeing; a girl walking alone, a Police Patrol van stopped when Zoya broke down. The Police took her home and hand over Zoya to her uncles' who were already randomly phoning her friends thinking she had eloped from home.

Zoya had no idea about what the Police told her family. Her uncles' wanted to keep it a secret and never lodged any complaint to protect the reputation of the family. Mita was found dead the next morning and all the remaining female members of her family left Bangladesh and moved to Silchar; Assam, neighboring India almost immediately leaving the male members to protect their land and interests until a settlement is made.

Zoya's rapist and abductors were never arrested and prosecuted, but her uncle accepted the compensation from the criminals and settled the matter.

Over the years; Zoya never remembered it until recently when she realized that she will never forget the assault, the pain and memories associated with it. She was a virgin before rape and she again felt losing control of her life and see her dreams crushing down.

CHAPTER 33

After fourteen months; Home Office refused Zoya's application with no right of appeal maintaining that she has not applied in time and did not provide the right documents covering at least the last two years indicating her cohabitation with Shan; there has been a gap from January to May and no documents addressed to either of them during this period.

Home Office asked Zoya either to leave the country immediately or they will take enforcement action against her at a suitable time.

Being stuck in nowhere; Ms Sen sent an ultimatum letter on her behalf to a particular legal department within the Home Office challenging the last decision, threatening to take them to the High Court, if the case is not reviewed and the last decision not withdrawn in the next fourteen days.

Unfortunately; the Home Office never acted promptly on Zoya's case as if it never took seriously Ms Sen's threat about taking them to High Court.

Zoya's frustration and repeated visits to Ms Sen's chamber lead to innumerable reminders being sent to the Home Office. As the time limit to lodge a Judicial Review at the High Court is three months from the date of decision and the last Home Office refusal was more than a year old, there was nothing in Ms Sen's capacity to speed up the matter but to wait patiently for any reply from the Home Office.

Meanwhile; Home Office passed Zoya's details to a private contractor, hired by them to pester people whose visas has expired; to leave the UK, by way of coercion and fear. They started sending letters directly to Zoya and called her a number of times scaring her that if she fails to depart voluntarily they will arrest and detain her and sent her back to Bangladesh by force.

Frantic Zoya changed her phone number, she also insisted that they change the house immediately. Shan was already planning to buy a new house, in the meantime; Dulal offered them free accommodation. Within two days the family packed and moved to the heart of Sylheti community in Oldham.

Zoya's apprehensiveness, lack of communication with the Bengali community for more than four years, uncertain immigration status and post traumatic stress syndromes meant she couldn't be the same socially friendly person again. Instead; struggling with reoccurring thoughts about the rape she suffered in Bangladesh, spending long hours in the house alone; she was in a state of hyper vigilance; easily startled and always anticipating another attack while living within her community. Nightmares, flashbacks, and sleep disturbances started disrupting her life. Constant efforts to avoid the memories of the trauma literally controlled her existence.

For reasons unknown; Zoya started disliking Dulal even more while living with him in the house, Shan's weird behaviour irked her the most; if lunch was five minutes late or he tripped over Raza's bicycle on the lawn, he'd fly into a disproportionate rage in front of Dulal. This dark side of Shan was new to her.

When the family moved to Dulal's house; Raza was at Year 4, at St Dunstan's Roman Catholic Primary School, he was a popular, well liked member of the school, he had many friends and was well thought of by his peers and adults alike. Despite his initial learning difficulties with help and support from his school and his mother at home, Raza always tried his best and worked hard at all times. He was enthusiastic about school life and participated in out-of-school clubs such as sports activities. As a child; growing up with the education from a mainstream Primary school, Raza had learned all the British values and was punctual, decent and had respect for everybody. Though the sudden decision of his parents to move house and take Raza away from school was not considered to be beneficial for him by his school peers, but there was nothing in their hands for the school to stop the move. Raza was the only ethnic minority pupil in the entire school and was a guinea pig; being forcibly recommended for therapy sessions. Though such rigorous assessment and tests actually had little impact on Raza's intelligence and ability but the school was successful to bring additional funds, in his name and there was no oversight on how the fund was spent.

The closest school to Dulal's house was Greenfield Primary which was already overcrowded and Raza didn't manage to get a place and he remained at home for a whole week which scared Zoya, thinking that her son's education will be hampered. Also; staying at home all day bored Raza, he was upset and irritated. However; Raza was quick to make friends with the children from next door but even they were at school.

It didn't took Raza any time to mingle with ethnic Bangladeshi children, moreover he was a no more the shy boy instead specialist inputs at his first school had already made him smart when compared with any average ethnic Bangladeshi boy of his age at the new school. The next door kids though born in the UK, struggled to speak English when Raza was accurate and fluent.

Raza was eventually offered a place at a nearby school; St Castilion Primary School and when the offer letter arrived; Zoya was stunned to see that the letter head of the school was printed bilingual; in English and Bengali.

The next day; Zoya and Shan took Raza to his new school where Zoya did not see any ginger hair child. Raza started school the next day and when Zoya went to drop Raza, immediately seeing a new face she was approached by other Bangladeshi women, curious to know about her. Already struggling with her mental health, Zoya failed to respond and her unresponsiveness was taken as an adverse quality. Zoya felt that the other parents were speaking about her in her back. Moreover; when other children were dropped off and picked up by their mother, father or any other family member in turn, in Raza's case, it was Zoya always.

Zoya could never communicate with other Bangladeshi Sylheti parents, most of them wear head scarf and long black overcoats at all seasons and the majority of the men had beards. On Fridays; the men particularly dressed up in traditional gear with a skull cap. Zoya felt disgusted, she desperately wanted to move Raza to a different school but her driving lessons had come to a halt, her passport retained by the Home Office and no visa granted meant her life was literally standstill.

Within the community Zoya tactfully avoided inquisitive approaches who wanted to know about the family, they having seldom interacted with Dulal before who was never at home.

However; Raza's friendship with the next door kids deepened, among the five younger children, the youngest two started spending majority of their time with Raza at the house. Though Zoya noticed Raza to be caring and friendly with the children but discovered Raza's toys and other items disappearing from home. She felt sorry for the boys and tried to explain them that it was wrong to take someone else's things without asking. Seeing; Raza's deep emotional bond with his friends, she became selfish and couldn't come down harshly on the children.

Raza was doing excellent at school, nobody raised any concerns, there was little homework and the progress was slow because majority of the students were unable to meet the target and parents didn't speak or write English and were of no help. However; it was the law in the UK that compelled reluctant parents to take the children to school fearing prosecution and loss of benefit payments.

Zoya could easily realize the downturn in Raza's progress and behaviour, he was becoming extremely rude and adamant. The regular lunch time fights at the playground between the groups meant that boys needed to be tough. There was extreme foul language always flying in the air, learnt by children at home from elder siblings. The playground was the most favourable place to vent out everything. Raza gradually got promoted within his group, defending their territory and the younger boys under their protection. During a crucial fight, as Raza was barred from the playground by the dinner lady, and his group had to withstand a bad defeat, extreme frustration lead to Raza run into the iron fence and banging his head, injuring him. An ambulance was called by the school; Zoya also received a call immediately and she ran to the school only to find Raza with a bandage on his forehead and the paramedics waiting for the mother to arrive. At the hospital; after three hours of various investigative tests and being cleared of any internal damage to his head, Raza was released.

That night; Zoya released her mistake of moving home and the impact of that on her son who was thriving at the previous school, she cried by herself and with no known remedy available, she struggled to stay positive.

The next day both parents were called at school for a meeting with the head teacher. Accompanied by Dulal when Shan and Zoya reached school at 12.30 pm, the clerk informed that the Head Teacher had left to attend a meeting at the Council Office and will not be available for that day. Hoping that they will be called for a meeting again, Zoya made up her mind to put up with a request for an assessment of Raza. She took out all the previous reports from the paediatric psychologist and other experts thinking that outside input will help Raza; otherwise he will be a spoilt brat. Unfortunately; Zoya and Shan were never called back; consequently; Zoya's ideas remained confined to herself when during a parent teacher meeting, she tried to raise the issue, it was airbrushed by the class teacher maintaining that Raza being one of the top performers in class, there is not a shred of doubt about his intelligence and ability.

Raza completed his primary school, Key Stage 3 with satisfactory results and got admission at a mainstream secondary mixed school; The Oldham Academy.

CHAPTER 34

Six years after her arrival into the UK, Zoya was served with enforcement papers by the Home Office and instructed to provide all relevant information in regard to her family circumstances prior to them making a final decision on her case; granting her leave or removing her from the UK.

Ms Sen made detailed submissions on Zoya's behalf, with evidence covering the entire six years, indicating her cohabitation with Shan and her son's academic records, photographs at school, in the summer camp, with friends in the community and letters from his primary and secondary school third party official confirmation about the involvement of Zoya in the upbringing of Raza, a minor British child in the UK. Raza also signed a letter drafted by Ms Sen on his behalf confirming his emotional bond and dependence on his mother and urging the authorities to allow his mother to remain in the UK, blaming the Home Office for not being able to go on a holiday in the last four years as his mother did not have her passport all this time and the mental agony he undergoes thinking about the prospect of his mother being removed from the UK and given his father's long working hours it is impossible for him to remain in the UK without his mother being present here.

Ms Sen was aware that despite the prescriptive nature of the new immigration rules whereby an applicant had to fulfill various criteria to become eligible under the family route depending on various parameters but the best interests of minor children; British or non British protected by another law enacted previously by the Parliament; based on international law obligation of the UK Government, previously ignored by the authorities was starting to get importance as more legal challenges were brought before the Courts and the same was scrutinized and explained by Judges in their own fashion with the sole intention to promote the welfare of children present in the UK, coercing the Home Office to give due regard to the statutory guidance to protect the interest of the children - a topic that can be elucidated in various ways and varied with individual circumstances of the child.

Ms Sen was certain that given Zoya's particular family situation involving her child, even if she is refused under the partner route, it was impossible for the Home Office to refuse her leave under the parent route. Most importantly;

the Statutory Guidance in regard to the children maintained that; wherever possible the opinion of the children concerned should be taken into account and Raza's letter detailing his family situation and involvement of his mother was impossible to overlook.

Soon after submitting the documents; Zoya received another letter from the Home Office directing to do a DNA analysis between Raza and Shan. When the letter arrived, nobody was at home and Zoya read it over and again to understand the meaning; seeing Raza and Shan's name mentioned, she became gripped with fear; thinking that if it comes to such a juncture, she will voluntarily leave the UK making an excuse, to see her mother on her death bed; suffering from cancer, to protect the interests of Raza. She could never imagine Raza leaving the UK and implications of that on him. Zoya felt empty and directionless, clutching the letter in her hand; she sat down in the sofa.

When Dulal and Shan arrived in the afternoon; they found Zoya lying unconscious on the sofa in the living room and the Home Office letter clutched to her hand. Dulal splashed water on her face and Shah started rubbing her feet frantically when suddenly she opened her eyes and finding herself in such a position, tried to sit up.

Dulal also read the Home Office letter which was addressed to Zoya but indicated that a DNA analysis must be made between Shan and Raza to establish her claim as a mother. Zoya was visibly upset since receiving the letter despite constant assurance by Shan and Dulal; something was pricking her and there was a visible gloom in her face.

Shan and Dulal being fully aware of her bizarre behaviour recently could not take a chance, the next morning; the trio went to Ms Sen's office for her opinion in the matter. Unfortunately; she was not there but her secretary insisted that Home Office has requested DNA analysis between Shan and Raza, however following Zoya's insistence; she said that Zoya's DNA can also be matched with Raza should she wishes to do so. She made all the relevant phone calls to the Home Office approved DNA analysis test laboratory in the UK, paying the fees for the DNA tests and providing the Test Centre with the details of the General Practitioner of the family. Ms Sen's secretary also informed Zoya and Shan to contact their GP with the Home Office letter; to inform them in advance about their intentions.

When Zoya and Shan showed the Home Office letter to their GP's secretary; she took it inside to the Doctor's Chamber and came back with the information that the DNA should be between Shan and Raza. She refused to include Zoya within it but Dulal's intervention in the matter; that Zoya wants to do it anyway outside of the Home Office request; at last satisfied the secretary and she agreed to register her name.

After receiving the kit from the DNA analysis laboratory; The GP's Surgery called them separately; first it was Shan and Raza and thereafter; Zoya.

The samples were separately forwarded to the laboratory. Two weeks after giving the swabs the result arrived at home; between Shan and Raza there was no match but Zoya and Raza's DNA matched perfectly.

When Dulal read out loud the results of the test and tried to explain the results to Shan; Zoya claimed mismanagement within the laboratory or when the samples were sent from the GP surgery.

Shan also blamed the wrong analysis method for the miss-match. After; Zoya and Dulal took the

DNA test result to Ms Sen; following a telephone enquiry by her with the Home Office, it was clarified that it was a typographical error and therefore Zoya and Raza's DNA analysis is mandatory not the other way round as indicated in the Home Office letter.

Therefore; Zoya and Raza's DNA test results showing (99.99%) match was immediately forwarded to the Home Office.

Zoya was granted settlement in the UK in December, just before she was due to complete seven years residence. Zoya was elated, it took her some time to realise the feeling of goodness. Everything seemed normal with the routine life she was used to but with a major change that she had no worries about her immigration status. Within a flick of a moment Zoya had all the rights and she could do everything legally which was not the case when she went to bed last night before the passport and letter confirming her status arrived.

Zoya also felt let down by the system, so much of her time was wasted by the delay and the last three years living with Dulal was most stressful for her. The same night Zoya couldn't sleep being kept awake by the thoughts of how to build up her life with her husband and son, suddenly she remembered Freddy and the good times they had together. For a moment; she thought of phoning him and giving him the good news. Last; she spoke to him was two years before when he confirmed having working for a clearing company in London.

CHAPTER 35

When Shan and Dulal came after midnight, Zoya was still awake and as Shan came upstairs to the bedroom she asked him not to return to the living room, she being keen to plan their future move already. Zoya wanted to speak with her husband in private but constant messages by Dulal on his phone and Shan's insistence that his help and knowledge is crucial to enable them to have a successful move meant that Zoya had to come down in the living room.

The low inflation economy and other people struggling to find a mortgage and the Government help to buy in partnership for first time buyers did not affect Shan, who had tirelessly worked year after year and saved up enough to make the move possible.

The dividends' he was receiving quarterly from his investment in the business was a fair amount and he having deposited the money in Zoya's account meant they can buy the property jointly.

The house hunting began the next day; Zoya left his driving instructor in the area, close to Stalybride where they had planned to find their dream home. She aimlessly moved from street to street looking for sale boards. Unable to find as many houses as she had expected she abandoned her search and went into the office of a local estate agent. Explaining her criteria; a decent four bedroom house with a fair size garden, Zoya was disappointed to know that the slow market conditions and steep competition in the area due to the close proximity from the town centre and all amenities, mean houses sell very quickly and four bedroom houses are rare to find.

Despite the negative input Zoya was not ready to give up, she offered the sales girl personal tip equivalent to the Estate Agents processing fees, if she can help her to find a house.

The girl craved in and took her mobile number promising that she will call her personally as soon as a house comes up in the area. Frustrated by the wait, after two weeks Zoya decided to take up the matter in her own hand. Every day after her driving lessons, with a notebook in her hand Zoya moved from street to street noting down street name, the house number and the estate agents contact number whenever she noticed a sale board. Her target was to find at least 20 houses and view them quickly within the next three days and decide before the end of the week.

After weeks of rekey Zoya found a prize house, it was an end of street property, a detached house surrounded by bosky countryside and had big reception rooms, four bedrooms and an annex.

Zoya instantly fell in love with it, the next day she again made an appointment with the Agent for a reviewing. When Zoya, Shan and Dulal came to view it, the Sales Agent told them that one buyer has already made an offer. Zoya immediately said that she is eager to quote £1000 above it. Dulal however; tried to dissuade her saying that until she passes her driving test, the move to the house will not be a practical one. Zoya gave deaf ears to his advice and the very next day she made an advance to secure the property.

After the legal proceedings were completed and Shan managed to take out a mortgage, Shan and Zoya were ready to move into their own house, an Edwardian house with a huge back garden and separated from the open farm lands by a narrow stream and woodland.

Shan and Zoya had no furniture, utensils or crockery except a 42 inch flat screen television set and a computer whatever they had in the first house was left behind. So; they required everything to be bought.

Dulal was distinctively not happy with the move but still assisted them to buy all the necessary things including the furniture. Zoya sometime thought him as a complex character beyond apprehension and childish. She understood that given the close friendship between Shan and Dulal and the family living together for more than 3 years was bound to bring sadness but she thought it was the right move before Dulal gets married and has his own family. Surprisingly; Zoya had never felt or seen Dulal's interest towards any women, she never felt uncomfortable with him.

The move went smooth; except that they had to book a local private taxi to take Raza to school. Zoya's regular input to pass her practical driving test became more rigorous; she booked the theory test and increased her lesson time to two and half hours every day.

One afternoon after coming back from her practical driving lesson, Zoya switched on the TV to watch the BBC news when suddenly she saw the flashing headlines at the bottom about the Polish man crushed to death by the collapse balcony of a flat in London.

In due course; Zoya was startled as Freedy's picture appeared on the TV screen identifying him by his name as the man who succumbed to his injuries and was pronounced dead at the scene when he was removing furniture from the flat with his colleague when the balcony craved in and he felt 30ft. Another man was seriously injured in the incident and admitted to hospital. Zoya couldn't believe that her only friend in the United Kingdom; is no more, that night she thought about his son, the little boy; Edmund who was hugely reliant on the money his father sent from the United Kingdom will now be in poverty. It took Zoya some time to overcome the grief.

CHAPTER 36

Zoya passed her theory test on the first attempt but she had to retake the practical test more than five times. On the first three tests, she failed for failing to read the road signs and was classed as a dangerous driver when she oozed passed a primary school, a 20 mile zone in 30mph speed. When her instructor informed that bumps at short intervals should make her alert as a 20mph zone, she managed to overcome the problem.

At last; Zoya passed her driving test, she was complemented as an excellent driver by the examiner, as she drove through the streets of Oldham; she being aware of all the curves and crevices. When the examiner declared the results she couldn't but stop herself and control her emotions and shook hands with the examiner and her instructor.

The same week; Dulal's old car was transferred to Zoya's name when he was about to buy a new car. When clearing the car boot Zoya was expecting to find some trash but instead, two handsome naked men with polished bodies looked at her seductively from the cover of a magazine. As she opened the little box; on the side, she uncovered more gay porn, videos and then condoms. As far as Zoya knew the car was only used by Shan and Dulal; Dulal was unmarried and they had never used condoms.

Zoya was clueless about homosexuality in Bangladesh; where such behaviour and identity is considered to be against Islam and demonic worthy of severe punishment and death if the person failed to correct himself.

While in the UK; when she was in college there were two English girls in the Maths class who lived together and she has watched them kissing and hugging in the toilet area. Later; she gradually understood that those of minority sexual identities, such as lesbian, gay, bisexual and transgender individuals had the right to engage in same-sex relationships without the fear of being persecuted and without losing respect within society here.

For her it was a waking nightmare; she refused to believe that Shan and Dulal could be in such a relationship. She felt tormented by many unanswered questions that automatically raised in her mind; whether it will be still possible for her to continue the relationship, whether Shan will admit or she should catch them, whether Shan had ever loved her, whether Shan was fantasizing about gay sex when they were intimate, what is wrong with her, is she unattractive, is she responsible for creating a gay husband?

She also thought about remaining in the closet and continuing as it was moving all these years, but constant flashbacks of Dulal's involvement with the family and his efforts to remain close to Shan all these years and managing to evade her suspicion meant; they under-estimated her intelligence and took her for granted when it was simply the other way round, her trust on her husband and considering Dulal as a younger brother of Shan; failure on her part to pick up the early signs made her feel like an idiot as she went through a wide range of emotions from devastation, shame, guilt, responsibility, and perhaps even to repulsion. She also thought that Shan may have felt that admitting the truth about himself would complicate things because of the stigma surrounding a gay husband in the Bangladeshi community and will led to the end of Dulal's brother-in-law's political career and ambitions relying on vote bank politics. Her confidence that her husband married her because he loved her made her pain more difficult.

Zoya was utterly unprepared for it, when Shan and Dulal came home in the afternoon, she couldn't confront them, and instead as she kept watching them together; it was amply evident that their relationship is beyond normal friendship between two males.

Zoya left the house around 3.00pm leaving them in the house to pick up Raza from school and by the time she returned they had already left.

In the evening; Zoya could not be in the living room; where Shan and Dulal spent time every night after coming from work, she went out in the back garden, walked past the stream and in the woods, it was a challenge for her to climb the steep hill but she continued until she reached a barren area, she was feeling mortified and wanted to kill herself, she tried to hang herself from a tree but fell down and fainted.

When Zoya regained her senses it was already late; she was feeling extremely weak, she returned home, the backdoor was still wide open and Raza was upstairs in his room busy playing interactive game with his friends on the internet.

Zoya had not eaten since morning; she made herself a cup of tea and few toasts, she regained her strength and tried to figure out her next course of action of how to tackle. Zoya made up her mind to catch them; she knew otherwise;

Shan will pretend innocence and it will be impossible for her to find out the truth though she begged to god that the truth should be otherwise.

That night; Zoya had made up her mind; she called Shan at half elevenish to find out how far they are telling him that she had a bad headache and she is going to sleep. Getting the information that they will reach in another ten minutes time, Zoya switched off the lights in the living room and waited, as soon as she heard Dulal's SUV pulling in front of the house, she run and hid in the closet under the stairs, holding the door knob from inside; waiting patiently.

Soon; she could hear Shan and Dulal talking and giggling nonstop alongside the sound from the television. Zoya; started feeling claustrophobic inside the closet; felt like time is not moving, she was not sure whether to come out or wait, her feet started aching. After a long wait; there was calm outside; except the sound of the television, she waited few minutes more and decided to come out. In a blink; she opened the closet door; saw there was dim light coming from the living room and the door was half closed, she gave a big leap and landed on the door opening it wide.

She saw Shan and Dulal naked standing, holding and rubbing their hardened black cocks and kissing each other. An unrecognised sound came out of Zoya; Shan and Dulal stood froze; obviously they didn't expect her at that time, being in that position. Zoya's voice trembled; she didn't know how to react. She started blabbering whatever came in her mind standing outside the living room door giving the men the opportunity to dress up. As Dulal was about to leave, Zoya ran into the kitchen grabbing the kitchen knife she came back and attacked Shan saying that she will kill both for destroying her life. Shan tried to stop her in empty hands sustaining a deep cut, there was blood oozing from his palm, seeing Zoya's fury, Shan also left home and Zoya remained standing in the porch holding the blood stained knife in her hand, she was utterly confused.

Zoya locked the door from inside and put the burglar alarm on, she managed to climb the stairs; her feet trembling and beyond her control, she went to the toilet washed her hand and the knife and fell into the bed.

CHAPTER 37

Zoya couldn't understand how to come to terms with the discovery that her husband is gay and he had been so for all these years, she had been in the UK and if it was not Dulal's carelessness, she would have never known the truth in her whole life.

Zoya remained laid with eyes open, she felt less bad to be left for the opposite sex rather than wondering what it was the "other man" had over her in the way of looks, physical attributes or sexual prowess. Unfortunately; she failed to understand that; such comparisons were inapplicable because Shan's bisexual character was not by choice. Of course; the close association with a homosexual may have triggered his particular trait. On the other hand, realizing that the person she married and for whom she decided to leave her country and spend almost a decade thinking; she knew him well - is not the person she married - nor did she know much about him –it was devastating. Zoya felt hurt and betrayed.

The next morning Zoya managed to dragged herself outside bed, her eyes were swollen and red, her voice coarse and her head heavy. She couldn't talk to Raza looking straight in his eyes blaming her for being so naive all these time. Zoya managed to drop Raza to school and returned home, whole day she sat in the living room thinking how to respond if Shan tries to contact or come home. She had no answer.

In the next few days and weeks; Zoya felt betrayed as she struggled to come to terms with the realty that she was deceived all these time by a complete lifestyle lie. She went through a wide range of emotions from devastation, shame, responsibility to repulsion. She struggled to decide whether to keep it a secret to escape the stigma surrounding a gay husband in the predominantly Bengali community. She knew that revealing the truth will have devastating consequences on Shan and others surrounding him.

With no effort from Shan or anybody to contact her actually made her feel guilty and somehow responsible. Had she been more possessive and inquisitive than whether it could have been avoided?

Weeks of mental agony and financial stress; her husband missing from home and she being entirely reliant on the savings, paying the mortgage and bills was becoming challenging. The only money she was getting; child benefit for Raza. Zoya lost substantial weight.

Ultimately; she legged to the local social security office; to find her options and she broke down when her caseworker advised her to see her General Practitioner (GP).Her GP did a sexual transmitted diseases (STD) screening with blood tests. The results came out with Zoya diagnosed with Hepatitis B positive and was prescribed a cocktail of medication.

Zoya was referred to Life Coach for counselling where a specially designed plan helped her enormously; to move forward. In the meantime; she started receiving financial support in the form of child tax credit, job seekers allowance and housing benefit. She enrolled herself at the local college to do further courses.

As she was gaining control; the urge to seek revenge was becoming prominent, more so; due to Shan's indifference towards Raza, who despite the very little involvement of his father in his life was missing him unknowing of the reason. When Zoya's efforts to contact Shan through a mediator to have contact with Raza; failed, she felt wounded, angry and hurt and was determined for revenge; taking matters in her own hands.

Morning after morning; once dropping Raza to school; Zoya went straight to Dulal's house and parking the car in the bend; she waited for hours but with no sign of Shan and Dulal in the horizon; she suspected the worst. Just before Easter; Zoya found a flyer at home with Rois' photo; an advertisement for the next general elections. He was being the consistent candidate winning the seat for almost two decades.

Zoya gathered strength and straightway went to Jalnupur Restaurant at Manchester town centre the next day. There was a party meeting going on and she was asked to wait. After two hours of waiting. A six feet tall, fair, skin head, suited man with fancy boots appeared; he spoke in Sylheti accent enquiring the reason for her urgency, Rois was startled when Zoya introduced herself. Thinking about her courage and audacity, he politely refused to give her any answer and remained indifferent. Zoya was boiling as she left the restaurant. She could easily feel the gender bias and sense of superiority of the man. She realised that he must have been instrumental in the disappearance of Shan and Dulal from the community fearing that if Zoya opens her mouth, it will malign his image and he was not ready to take any chance.

That afternoon; when Zoya reached Oldham; she went straight to the main Mosque near to Dulal's house and demanded to speak to the Chief priest. She discussed the immoral acts of her husband involving 'a kafir' and direct links to a political leader. She managed to paint an extreme sorry picture. The Imam promised to help her.

The following Friday; orders were issued secretly in all the Mosques; not to vote for Rois leading to a humiliating defeat to him and his decision to leave Oldham for good.

CHAPTER 38

Zoya again studied English as a second language (higher level) at the college. While at college; she performed a traditional dance she learned as a child, on the cultural diversity day.

She later auditioned and was selected to perform at the ceremony for the Learning and Skills Improvement Service Star awards, which was held in London every year when her teacher; Lynn was nominated for an award.

When Raza was in Year 10; Zoya managed to find full-time work as a welfare support worker at Oldham City Council. After initial training and working under a Manager; she was given the job to work with; around 100 families in Coldhurst and Shaw. Apart from that she helped out in schools and nurseries, interpret for Bangladeshi families at medical and dental appointments, and encourage them to get involved in community activities.

The big house; with a huge interest only mortgage payment, the bills and other living expenses were so high, Zoya gradually found her entrapped in a situation which was impossible to break, with a teenager son, she never had the money to have yearly holidays to Bangladesh.

Immediately upon arrival; Zoya missed so many things; her friends, the joint family, the politics within it, she being extremely favourite to her eldest uncle's wife, the fish curry, the dry fish preparations, very hot chilies' and vegetables grown in Bangladesh; particularly the special lemon used in almost all preparations; everything seemed so tasteless here. Zoya also missed the riverside, the rains, and the smell of the soil after the first rainfall. The blazing hot summer months and the soft winter sun but gradually over time; particularly the initial long delay and the messing up of her case by the Home Office forced her to forget the past. The upheavals in her personal life and the struggle that followed discarded all contact with Sylhet. The pressure from her family back home for marriage also dissuaded her enormously. The only remaining contact she had with Sylhet was over the phone and as years passed she gradually lost all her family members one by one, year after year. By the time; Raza completed his A levels and moved to London, to study Business and IT at London University; there was nobody left in the family; except her cousins.

However; over the years; Zoya started loving the country, except the initial experience with the Home Office, she found being treated equally. Had access to education opportunities and work that helped her to survive all these years. The passing of the driving test; gave her that independence, she wanted for a long time.

As a single mother; she tried her best to raise her son to British values and as an Asian; she gave utmost importance to his education and encouraged him at all times. When Raza's favourite food became yorkshire pudding, cakes and chocolate, Zoya also stopped cooking at home and became reliant on ready meals; just adding more spices to them.

Before; Zoya could realize she started dying her hair to cover the greys', she still remembers the more specific days; she attended Raza's graduation ceremony in London; wearing the suit she purchased from Next Store.

The day; Raza phoned to inform that he has found someone through an internet match making site and is now seeing her regularly. Zoya couldn't wait to meet Yasmin; she was garrulous with a cockney accent. When Zoya went to meet her parents in the cramped house at Tower Hamlet Borough, she struggled to tackle the questions concerning Raza's father and his whereabouts. Zoya was unsure how much Raza knew about Shan's secret life. Despite; Shan's rudimentary involvement in Raza's life; he was upset immediately after his father's disappearance from home, his mother's failure to give a satisfying reply gradually created the grievance within him; blaming both parents. All these years; Zoya had never told Raza about his father's sexual behaviour and the reason behind him leaving home for good without bidding good bye to Raza.

As they walked down Brick Lane; Zoya for the first time opened her mouth, they sat in the small park opposite Aldwich Tube Station and Zoya started speaking telling every bit of what she saw that fateful night; his father left the house and never to return.

Zoya couldn't figure out Raza's feelings after knowing the truth, he remained calm and said that he will try to locate his dad after all these years. On her return journey; Zoya was kept occupied by the thoughts of how everything changed within a span of less than a few minutes that fateful night she found Shan and Dulal. Many ideas raced through her mind; whether she had acted too harshly, how deep was the cut in Shan's hand, whether she could have murdered him that night if he had stayed back, whether she would have accepted him if he had come back to the house, whether they would have still be in Manchester if she would have not involved the religious and community leaders. The idea came that she was responsible for destroying Rois' life as well. The Restaurant Jalnupur has since changed hands many times with different names and Zoya was unaware of the new name.

She thought of trying to somehow contact Rois and obtain information about Shan; but she didn't know where to begin with; after all these years.

The next step Zoya took was to apply for a divorce through a Family law Solicitors who assured her that the Court will find the whereabouts of her husband through Council Tax notification and will serve the Notice when Zoya will become aware of his address. After a painstaking wait; nothing came back from the Solicitors except that her husband is untraceable.

Zoya was compelled to take a different approach, she managed to get the name of Rois' elder brother's restaurant in Helston from a waiter who worked at Jalnupur Restaurant during the initial years. Searching on the internet; she found the restaurant; still located in

Helston and is part of a group called; Stable Restaurants Ltd.

Zoya decided to travel to Helston; she took the Virgin train to Newport and the local train from there arriving in Helston; Cornwall. It was late evening; Zoya went straight to a local hotel and for dinner she went to Ali's Restaurant. She was again disappointed; Ali had sold off the business to his step brother Aklas and is managing the new restaurant at the town centre. Zoya had no time to waste and she had no intention to give up. She managed to meet up Ali at the restaurant. Ali was taken by surprise; Zoya neither displayed any reluctance nor was hesitant to tell the truth, all she wanted was information about Dulal and Shan.

But Ali seemed reluctant; looking at his face; Zoya could see that he had learnt the truth for the first time about Rois' decision to return to his family in Helson which he initially took as the coming out from the spell of his wife and returning to his brother, something Ali considered his triumph over his sister-in-law. Rightly; it was revealed how wrong he was. However; Rois didn't lived in Helston for long, he moved to the suburb of London; in Redding and continued with his socio- political activity.

Ali couldn't give any information about Dulal; but assured Zoya that he will try to find out somehow without revealing anything about Zoya's visit and will pass on the message as soon as he will get any information.

Though it was nothing of Ali's interest but hearing Zoya's story, he developed extreme compassion for her and took it up as a challenge. Ali knew that his brother will never share any information about Dulal with him knowingly and he waited for the opportunity. Ali initially tried to gather information from Rois' staff members, as a naive; eager to know about another family member who has lost contact.

Days of trying the same trick ultimately yielded result when another Sylheti Bangladeshi recruited in the election campaign took up his bait and replied that though he had never personally met Dulal but there was a phone call for Rois few days back; from one Dulal in Helsinki, Finland and he had answered the call and he managed to get the number.

Ali immediately phoned Zoya and pass her the telephone number; presumably from Dulal. Zoya gave Raza the number and asked him to call.

CHAPTER 39

It has been more than twenty five years; but Raza's memory was still fresh of his father and Dulal uncle, despite the estrangement and detachment he was very much a part of the family from the very day he arrived here. He still remembered seeing Dulal uncle with his dad all the time; in fact he has seen his dad spending all the time with him as far his memory went. He also remembered Dulal uncle talking the family for outings; taking him to medical appointments and his helping attitude all the time and even allowing to live in his house for quite a few years.

But then one morning; Raza came down and found his mum sitting with red eyes in the front room, in the new house and he had since not seen his dad or Dulal uncle. Initially; Raza was too busy with his own life and didn't understand the loss. His mother was evasive; she never said anything and maintained she does not know their whereabouts. Raza at times thought the new house unlucky and blamed it on his mother for insisting his dad to buy it.

As a violent aggressive teenager; Zoya struggled as a single mother; to bring up his son but she never lost patient that ultimately paid off.

The bashing of the doors, long hours of internet gaming, ignoring his studies, peer pressure on his son to achieve everything what others have; made her worried but somehow she managed everything efficiently.

Raza had never bothered about his father; he had never actually missed him in his life; he was never there for him. Something that did bother him; as a teenager, at high school when on Parents- Teachers Meeting Day; all other boys had their father with them running from room to room, with him it was his mother. His mother had always said that even if he was present; he wouldn't have attended; a shy man with no knowledge of English would have been more embarrassing for him. In high school; some bully's tried to have a go on him calling him; " son of a $hit stabber", though he didn't understand the significance, at that time but his reputation as 'a black belt in Taekwondo' and his fists of anger and fights gave him enormous protection. However; once finishing school; he simply ran away from Oldham.

Now; after all these years knowing the truth about his father hardly made any difference to Raza. Upon his mother's insistence; he decided to make the call to Dulal.

After a long wait; somebody on the other end answered in a feeble voice; the voice was fade and coarse; after few minutes of reserved conversation Raza revealed himself; 'Dulal uncle it's me; Raza' there was no expression of any feelings from the other side, except wanting to know the reason for his call. Raza tried to beat the bush telling it had been impossible to find the telephone number; maintaining that it was not entirely his fault and how much he missed his father all these years. Dulal uncle was a patient listener; however; as he revealed that it is very important that he speaks to his dad. When enquired the reason for the urgency; Raza's response was vague except that he is yet to marry and the embarrassment his mother had to undergo at the bride's family home.

When; Dulal uncle said the truth that he had been really late and Shan can longer be contacted or spoken; only he can come and visit his grave and take whatever that is rightfully his; and he is tired of being the custodian. Raza couldn't make up his mind whether to tell his mother or go to Finland and find out everything by himself. But when Zoya called that night; Raza couldn't lie and he said; it's a bit too late; father is no more and buried in Finland. Raza also disclosed about Dulal uncle's invitation to him to come to Finland and take hold of everything that belonged to his father.

Zoya mumbled and asked Raza's opinion in the matter; as Raza struggled; he being in double minds whether he actually had the moral authority to inherit his father's possessions, Zoya; in fact provoked him; saying that Dulal uncle has rightfully stated; at least this way he can compensate for all his wrongdoings, Raza could feel the hatred spewed out of her as she spoke her mind. Raza didn't blame her, however; he made up his mind to visit Helsinki.

As the plane hovered over Helsinki airport; on a clear late evening, contrary to his expectations Raza saw a large, dense, urban area below full of lights and stretching for miles. Looking up; he could see a thousand stars and constellations. Raza came outside of the airport and noticed a bearded man holding a placard by his name, introducing himself as Ata Turk; a Turkish immigrant, the taxi driver sent by Dulal uncle, to take Raza to his house.

Raza sat beside the driver sit, keeping his suitcase and hand bag in the back seat; almost immediately they took to the maze of streets and within minutes landed on the abyssal pitch dark highway with cars chasing in high speeds more than 150 miles per hour and the flashing headlights. Raza felt nervous; he never had experience of travelling in such high speed in the UK where the maximum speed on the motorway is 70mph. He felt like being in a racing car and held his breath; didn't want to distract the driver so decided to keep mute.

After two and half hours of running; the car took a side road that relieved Raza as he made up his mind to take the train during the return journey.

Travelling within the suburb was a normal experience; after a few blocks the taxi pulled off in front of a huge house with a small gate and a side entrance. As; Mr. Turk opened the back door to take out his luggage; and Raza came out and stood in the footpath; almost immediately he noticed the side door opened and a shadow; calling his name; Raza walked towards him. He couldn't believe his eyes; to the extent Dulal uncle's health has deteriorated; he gave him a light hug, took the luggage from Mr. Turk and walked inside.

The wooden stairs fell on a huge landing area with a large shoe cabinet and a wooden seat that led into an area of common passage with two large living rooms; filled with comfortable, tan leather couches, colourful rugs over the bare wood floor, and a large display case with pictures, books, and many memories, his father almost in every picture.

On one side there was a huge bedroom with fitted wardrobes and on the other side there is a huge kitchen and dining area and a toilet. Raza and Dulal uncle had dinner together and Dulal uncle said that this will be his flat and he can all use it by himself till everything is sorted and the next door property belongs to his father.

Raza was awakened by the sound of tram just outside the bedroom window early in the morning. He couldn't go back to sleep; so wake up to make himself some morning tea. After having tea; Raza found some Danish sausages and eggs in the fridge and bread in the breadbox, everything neatly arranged within the kitchen. He fried some eggs but didn't toast the bread for he didn't want it to go cold and waited for Dulal uncle.

Dulal uncle came from outside after a while; with a salad dish in his hand and they sat down for breakfast; the vegetables and baby lettuces are from the garden. As far as Raza remembered; Dulal uncle was a charming talkative lively person; his transformation to this quite old man in his late sixties; was unimaginable. Though he appeared looking healthy but there was a shroud of sadness in his face.

Immediately after breakfast; Dulal uncle took a handful of drugs; Raza couldn't help but ask the reason; when to his surprise he replied that this are the live sustaining medications for him; to keep his immune system balanced; he being Hepatitis B positive and has liver cirrhosis.

Looking at Raza's facial expression that looked anguished; Dulal uncle smiled and said; he knew it will be shocking for him; so he has arranged everything separately for him. He also assured that regular intake of the drugs will give him a long healthy life.

After; breakfast Dulal uncle gave him a bunch of keys for the next door house; and a File containing a will and the papers of the house but everything written in Finish. Raza wanted translations. Dulal uncle gave him an address and asked him to go to their office at the City Centre; for translations. The house was situated in such a convenient location with the tram running from just outside; all destinations were easily reachable. Raza took the tram to town centre and managed to locate the translation office run by an English man. He handed over photocopies of the documents and paid some advance. He was asked to return after three days.

Raza had lunch outside; since; hearing about the Hepatitis B diagnosis; he had a feeling of weariness, he didn't want to believe in the first place; having grown up with the stigma associated with it. However; Dulal uncle seemed quite used to his condition and determined to keep it under control. He made up his mind not to disclose it to his mother; as it will unnecessary make her more worried.

Upon his return; Raza thought of going to his father's house; but then decided to wait for Dulal uncle and go with him the first time; unfortunately Dulal uncle was nowhere to be seen and Raza dozed off in the sofa; until he was awakened by a knock on the door. It was Dulal uncle and together they went to the house next door.

Between the two houses there was no boundary wall; Raza could see the garden tidy with vegetable patches and huge bags of compost with fruit trees planted in them. The house also had a side entrance and the door opens into a lobby with a kitchen and huge living room. The furniture was old dated and there were two bedrooms upstairs. There was a medium sized cellar which required decoration and repair.

Compared to Dulal uncle's four storey house; basement and three storey up; his father's house was small but there was a large stretch of land in the front and at the back of the house.

The house was not as well kept as that of Dulal uncle's; but it was reasonably in order. Again; almost all displayed photographs were Dulal uncle and his father; in different locations and in jubilant mood. Suddenly; Raza felt a sense of being overlooked by the man; had a similar feeling of rejection like his mother and his eyes became heavy.

Though; Dulal uncle was insisting that he should stay back and sort out the things; Raza was in no mood and felt the urgency to leave the house immediately; by running away from everything associated with the man whose life was a deceit.

Seeing his somber mood; Dulal uncle understood the reason of his agony and left him alone to have some mental retrospection and gaining control over his emotions as he was required to go through some arduous tasks.

Raza tried hard to cope with the battle raging inside him; to ignore everything and return to the UK, since he didn't came to Finland for the money and visible avoidance of him by his father all these years; made him felt no one to the dead man and he wanted to reject his will. Raza didn't feel hungry; there were ready meals on the fridge but he was tried and sleepy.

Raza went to bed; the next morning he was fresh with the idea imprinted on his head that all this legally belongs to him, he being the legitimate heir and it was not his fault that his parents separated and his father left the country and never tried to contact him. In fact; it was he who is the real sufferer; not anybody else.

After having breakfast; Raza straightway went to the house next door; he had made up his mind to start sorting out things; beginning from his bedroom; first he opened the bedside drawers, on the top one, he found; hoards of medication with strange names and on the drawer below there were nail clippers, cough drops, and the usual miscellany. He took out the entire drawer and turned it upside down on the bed sheet in the floor, there was nothing of value to him. But when Raza started emptying the closet; he uncovered gay porn, videos and then condoms.

All the clothes were aged except a very few amongst them there was a Superdry Jacket that fitted Raza perfectly; leaving that aside; Raza dumped all the clothing in separate black liners, he had no sad realizations or hesitations except the weird feeling that he never thought in his life time that he will be doing so.

Extremely fade-up with the monotonous job; he started using his hand to scoop out everything from the shelves jammed with hoards of paper and photographs on the floor and as Raza started quickly clearing up the floor; he found the album; with family photos; taken on a variety of times; ranging from the day; he landed at Heathrow; clinging to his mum; at the first house; when he couldn't speak a word of English, the Moors; at various shopping centre's; all must have been taken by phone or he had faint memories of pictures clicked by Dulal uncle. As Raza; was holding the album upside down; one of the pictures fail out and he saw the year written on the back of it; curiously; he checked and found that all of them had the year written on the back and some have dates. He found pictures of his birthday celebrations; at Dulal uncle's house and the next door children in it. Raza couldn't remember all their names; wandering where they are?

The discovery gave him solace; at least he had not forgotten them all but kept the memories preserved in the best way he could. Keeping; the album aside; Raza placed everything for disposal; not even bothering to look to the paperwork; if any of them is of any value.

The next room closet was almost empty; except few shoes and overcoats that was cleared easily. Clearing the living area was uneventful. But entering the kitchen for the first time; Raza found the worktops quite high; given the low height of his father; he kept thinking how he managed using the kitchen, in the corner; he found two foot stool's that must have been in use all the time. The kitchen cabinets were full with various spices, groceries, crockery, utensils, pressure cookers and large reserves of fat rice, oil and flour.

Raza was occupied by the thought of the monumental task still left; as he decided to end the job for the day and return to Dulal uncle's house. It was late afternoon; and Dulal uncle couldn't be found anywhere. Raza warmed up a ready meal and had his lunch. Dulal uncle returned after a while and joined him to watch television.

Raza tried to pick up a conversation; but it was extremely difficult; the man had changed so much since the time; he last saw him in England. He hardly talks now-a-days except short scripted answers to questions put forward to him and limited information and advice; to enable Raza to pack up his business, in Finland smoothly. But; Raza had made up his mind to know everything about what happened after the night they left home; his dad bleeding badly from his hand.

CHAPTER 40

Opening up was difficult for Dulal uncle; initially; but gradually he became more at ease; though initially confused; they rushed to A&E at Oldham hospital where Shan repeatedly lied about the injury telling that he asked a colleague to throw the knife towards him during busy time in the kitchen; and he injured the palm by trying to catch a flying sharp knife.

The Indian doctor; Registrar at the A&E looked in disbelieve but wrote what Shan said in the medical notes. They cleaned, stitched and bandaged the hand. They returned home early morning and didn't know what to do whether to apologize to Zoya and end it all for good or just run away.

Dulal was very scared about his brother-in-law's political career; in such a sensitive minority area where any rumor about the sexual orientation of his family member would be fatal to his political career. The stigma associated with it was enough to end the social and community ties of her sister and brother-in-law within the tight knitted predominantly Muslim Bangladeshi community who will not hesitate to ostracize them.

Shan couldn't go to work the next day; his hand had swollen and he was in real pain, Shan's absence had a major impact on the busy night; he being the head chef. Dulal; had tried in vain to find a chef earlier the day to replace Shan. In the evening everything went wrong and it descended into chaos as the trainee chef couldn't supply the orders.

When Rois came at 11.00 pm to collect the earnings; unhappy customers were still lingering and complained to him about all sorts of disorders from extensive long waiting period to wrong tasteless dishes being served, the rice was uncooked and the grilled meat was half cooked.

Only; Rois could apologize and charge one-third of the price for the orders. When; he wanted to know from Dulal the real reason; he told him that Shan had a terrible fight at home with his wife and he has injured his hand. Rois was extremely disappointed and wanted to meet Shan, but Dulal stopped him giving the excuse of his terrible mental state stating that things will soon be alright.

The next day; Rois managed to get a replacement chef; on a high wage to keep his restaurant running smooth. After; a week Shan's injury was still raw causing suspicion to the doctors who immediately recommended blood tests. The test results identified Shan as diabetic with very high levels of blood sugar.

Given the deteriorating condition of his hand injury; he was immediately referred to the diabetic centre at Manchester Royal Infirmary where while giving his individual history; Shan revealed his sexual identity officially; as 'a bisexual'. Immediately; further blood tests were conducted and two weeks after leaving home; Shan was declared as HIV positive and Hepatitis B positive. Both Shan and Dulal were flagged to the Consultant in GU Medicine at Manchester Centre for Sexual Health. Surprisingly; Dulal was tested negative for HIV but was found to be Hepatitis B positive. Doctors were astounded by the discovery and requested for Dulal's consent for his blood samples to be sent to the research laboratory for further evaluation; to find any possible hint about the compound in his blood or the DNA that protected him from HIV.

Shan's viral load was found to be very high and his CD count was low; he was prescribed anti-retroviral drugs and medication for his Hepatitis B viral load, he was straightway admitted to hospital and put on intravenous Insulin.

However as weeks passed and Shan's hand injury didn't improve instead the gangrene started spreading, doctors decided to perform an amputation of his right hand up to the wrist. Dulal was on his side all the time at hospital and hardly went home. It was a major decision; the psychological impact on Shan; was devastating. But; as the last resort; doctors decided to go with the operation and assured him that with the right help, training and equipment he will bounce back to a normal life. Immediately after losing his hand down the wrist; the emotional loss was tremendous but Shan's physical recovery was quick that brought in a sense of relief.

While Shan was in hospital; business at Jalnupur started plummeting; with the general elections approaching it was becoming extremely hard for Rois to manage the campaign and business in one go. Dulal always dissuaded him from visiting Shan at the hospital; taking the responsibility on himself and assuring him that his wife is taking good care of Shan.

Until; Zoya visited Jalnupur before Easter and wanted to know the whereabouts of Shan; thinking that she might have a different agenda and making a fool of him; Rois refused to give any answer and despite her threats simply asked her to leave.

That afternoon; Rois went to see Shan at the hospital when he took Dulal in the cafe downstairs and wanted to know the truth; Dulal remained mute but his silence spoke for himself.

Rois proposed that as soon as Shan is discharged from hospital they should leave the UK for good and he will help them to resettle in any European country. The next day; 'a Sale Board' went up on Dulal's property and flight tickets were booked for Helsinki; for the same day Shan was due to be discharged from hospital.

Dulal collected his own and Shan's medical history and a specific referral letter for them to the State Hospital in Helsinki. They boarded the Finnish Airlines Flight from Manchester; on Thursday; travelling straight from the hospital with few belongings.

Immediately upon arrival they checked in a hotel; with sunlight averaging 19 out of 24 hours' Shan and Dulal had few sleepless nights when they moved to a small flat outside the city centre, few days later. Long heavy dark curtains put of the bedroom window; at last helped them to create a dark atmosphere. Shan had his first dressing at the Finnish hospital where a Nigerian English speaking nurse was of great help.

Dulal had already opened the bank account for Rois to put the money; to open a small business to survive. The money arrived after almost three months; Dulal and Shan also came to know about Rois' defeat in the elections and Zoya going public in the community; and Dulal's family being ostracized; and their move out from Oldham.

When Jalnupur was sold Shan got his proportionate share amounting to two hundred fifty thousand pounds, however; Dulal's house did not fetch much profit but still between them they had enough money to start a small cafe.

In the meantime; Shan had an artificial hand fitted and he was under training from physiotherapists and occupational therapists to use it efficiently.

Almost; a year after their move to Helsinki; Shan and Dulal managed to open the cafe; on the main square at the city centre; where they served hot food (fusion dishes invented by Shan)and sold drinks and cannabis illegally.

Not so long after; Shan's creations became the talk of the city as more and more Fins got the taste of curry powder. It remained jam-pack on weekends and during lunch times, every day. Dulal served the food and counted the money when Shan prepared it singlehandedly. They hardly returned home during day-time; leaving around 9 am in the morning and opening the cafe at 12 noon. The addition; of a Pakistani illegal immigrant; Akram, who had entered Finland from Russia; en-route to the UK; was enormously helpful to Shan.

Akram worked in the kitchen, slept at the cafe and did almost everything, he got used to the life so much that he gave up his idea to make it to UK and decided to remain in Finland and ultimately got settled through marriage.

Unlike; the Chicken Tikka Masala in the UK, Shan's Garlic Tikka Masala; became popular with the customers in Finland; it was not sweet but spiced 'hot' and as a mild curry dish; Butter Chicken was liked by many. Between these two dishes more than 1000 dishes were sold a week. In the afternoon; the Indian tea and Indian coffee with cardamom became very popular.

The routine life continued for the next twenty years; despite their specific medical conditions and Shan's uncontrollable diabetes; as he was unable to control his diet.

In regard to their sexual life; as partners; the busy schedule and aging brought in natural inhibitors; knowing that Shan was HIV positive made Dulal more hesitant; for long they struggled to figure out the source of the infection and blamed it on a Canadian man they had befriended at the Night club; in Manchester. Shan; also had the bizarre theory of having contracted the virus from Dulal who passed it on to him without himself getting infected which grew stronger with time and there was nothing in Dulal's capacity to change the belief.

When they retired; Dulal brought the house; it was big enough for them to share and they started growing lots of vegetables and fruits; Shan being extremely knowledgeable about it. He started growing exotic vegetables; like pumpkins, bananas in the conservatory and once managed to grow corn plants in a small patch.

When the next house was put on sale; Shan wanted to buy it despite; Dulal's discouragement; when for the first time; he mentioned about his son; telling that he had a moral duty to leave something for Raza; expressing the guilt he carried all his life for not saying goodbye to him before leaving the UK.

It was impossible for Dulal to understand such emotional ties as he had none but he wholeheartedly supported Shan and the purchase was made.

CHAPTER 41

Shan moved to his new house; rearranging the furniture with which it was sold; the kitchen top was too high for his height but he didn't put a new kitchen instead used foot stools and stand on them for cooking and washing dishes. Dulal; was annoyed by his miserly behaviour, thinking about the risks he is talking for few grants that could endanger his life.

To discourage him from using the kitchen; every morning Dulal called him over to his house and they spent the days together, making sure that he returned to sleep and the same routine continued for almost four years. After retirement; they also had regular frequent holidays to various European countries except the UK and Russia; for fear of homophobia.

Since; the last two years Shan also started attending the Mosque every Sunday mornings and one January Sunday morning; he fell ill with chest tightness and nausea while at the Mosque and was transferred to hospital when blood tests revealed advanced renal failure; he having developed side effects of Tenofovir; the anti retroviral drug. Immediately; his treatment was changed to Abacavir, Darunavir, Ritonavir and Dolutegravir to counteract the side effects of Tenofovir on his kidneys. In addition; a biopsy showed nephropathy and he was commenced on heamodialysis three times a week. Shan was also commenced on a new medication to treat his Hepatitis B. With such complex drug regime and regular dialysis; Shan became morally low day by day and he plunged into a crippling depression, never to revive and drift away into a fantasy land of zombies, ghost and what not-carrying the version of depression-Schizophrenia; he started avoiding Dulal and ultimately declared break up-following a direct conversation with God, overpowering the Satan.

Breakup wasn't easy for Dulal, getting over was hard, there was no quick fix to heal the heart fast, but he learned the ways to lessen the heartache by secretly following Shan and watching him from a distance.

It was during these secret follow ups, Dulal discovered Shan in one of the most unexpected of the places; the death cafe; where often strangers, gather to eat cake, drink tea and discuss death.

Though Death Cafe organisers portray it as a non-profit organisation with no intention of leading people attending it to any conclusion or course of action but Dulal found it pungent when attending the same and participating on a group discussion on 'suicidal intentions', he found the discussion provocative and directional.

Then came that fateful day; when at night Shan took an overdose of insulin and lay dead; in the house. When not getting a glimpse of him the entire morning and Dulal's telephone calls remaining unanswered; he called the Police; who had to do a force entry to the house; Shan was found lying on the bed, an open insulin pen lying on the floor and a folded paper on the bedside drawer. Police sealed the room and took the body for post- mortem. Dullal had to call a locksmith to repair the main door. He knew; Shan was depressed and waiting for something like this to happen. He regretted for not being trying to help him before; despite his rejections. After all; he was the only companion Shan had. Two days later; the Police arrived and handed over Shan's suicide note to Dulal, as it was specifically addressed to him.

When Dulal went through the heartbreaking letter; he found how much Shan was suffering physically and mentally following self introspection; blaming himself for destroying lives and looking at his ailments as a punishment for his actions; which was in a sense true and in the end; he wanted to escape from the sufferings; all misdeeds; deception that he had committed since leaving his simple life in Sylhet. His tone was somber and there was enormous confusion within him, as he feared punishment but ultimately the physical suffering made it unbearable for him and he decided to end it all by himself. He also; apologized to Dulal for his rudeness in the end; giving the justification, otherwise; it would have been impossible to part. In the end; he put the responsibility on him to handover everything he possessed to Raza and requested to give him a Muslim burial. Dulal liaised with the Hospital mortuary and contacted the Mosque officials to collect his body; to do the rituals prior to his burial as per his wishes.

Shan's funeral took place at the Mosque where Dulal was not allowed to be present but he patiently waited outside and took part in procession and was present until everything was done and Shan was made to rest in peace. When; everyone had left; Dulal gave a silent mindful ovation to the indomitable spirit.

After Shan's death Dulal never entered his house; but did all the necessary things as the custodian of his Will; and when his efforts to contact Raza was not materializing; he even was planning to travel to the UK for the purpose and telephoned his brother-in-law; Rois.

Dulal uncle also mentioned; about a box left in the attic for Raza and keys on the top of the boiler in the kitchen. Realizing that his father had an agonising end; Raza felt extremely sorry for him, it was not his fault for being different; the only injustice he did was towards his mother.

However; Raza expressed his desire to visit the grave and next day Dulal uncle took him to the huge cemetery outside town; where Raza could only see headstones of varied sizes and wild flowers of different colours blooming; on the golden spring day with butterflies and bees blithely quivering in the air, impatiently and spontaneously.

Dulal uncle was struggling uphill and Raza scrambling behind, suddenly realizing seeing aimless arthropods that spontaneity has a specific rhythm and rhyme of its own, and that natural emotion has a normal playful pace and it behaves like a wayward butterfly flying in a not-so- strong whirlwind. He realized that it is a pleasure to sing out in unison with nature's concert, he had an ecstatic feeling.

On reaching the top; he moved his eyes around, spell-bound; the dark blue sea and the skyline meeting at infinity; the water dotted with ships taking men on their real life journeys; while his father lays at rest.

It was an unmarked grave; with no headstone and would have been impossible for him to found; without Dulal uncle's help.

As Dulal uncle strolled forward destroying the wild flowers; carelessly looking at the open sea. Raza stood in the front; he felt an enormous sense of loss; in his life for not doing anything to find the real man, 'a brave soul' who despite the rejections didn't forget about his son. He murmured the prayers of forgiveness.

Raza couldn't control his emotions; wiping his eyes; Dulal uncle put a hand on his shoulder and uttered that the soul is never born; neither never dies; at any time; nor does it come into being; again when the body is created; the soul is birth less; imperishable; timeless and is never destroyed when the body is destroyed.

Dulal uncle asked Raza to sit beside the grave and he took few photographs with Raza's mobile phone.

They hardly talked to each other while on the three hour journey back home. But Raza somewhat liked the fondness exhibited by this man; he had all his life thought as his real enemy for destroying his life.

Raza understood that it was not in his father's capacity to alter his sexual orientation; if wouldn't have been Dulal uncle; it would have been someone else. But; why then he married mum; was a million dollar question for which he never had an answer.

CHAPTER 42

The next morning; Raza left home early; going to the translators office first; collecting the translation of the Will, he scanned and emailed it to a Property Solicitors, in White Chapel; London; he was in liaise with to first read and advice him before signatures.

He was further required to make an Affidavit confirming his acceptance and agreeing to all terms before the house is transferred to his name and the money held in a Finish bank could be transferred to his bank account in the UK. Without nodding from his legal advisers in the UK, Raza was keen to wait. When he rang the Principal's Office in London; they gave a timeframe of at least 48 hours before making any comment. Nonetheless; Raza instructed the attorney's office to liaise with the Charitable Trust and the Local Authorities; to purchase the lease of the piece of land; where his father was buried.

In the meantime; he decided to sort out the house; Dulal uncle had told him that the house clearance people will only remove everything in one go and if they had to come back again for anything; it will be chargeable.

The next bedroom closet were all full of bills of variety; electric, water, gas and council rates, all jumbled together but kept since the house was purchased. Raza had nothing to sort between them but bag them all. The living room was sorted easily. Only; sorting out the kitchen was time consuming and it took an entire day. Except the few crockery all the pots were dented and marked and were bagged for the bin. The shelves packed with spices most of them outside the expiry date were bagged away. A whole cupboard was full of seeds of many shapes and sizes in small bottles which Raza packed separately for Dulal uncle.

On the top of the boiler in the kitchen; Shan found the two keys in a keychain. He took it and walked up to the attic door and unlocked it; there was pitch darkness inside and Raza felt cold. Using his mobile phone; he turned on the light switch; it was an empty room, carpeted with a wooden box in one side and two roof windows tapped with black sticker from the inside.

Raza sat on the carpet and used the other key to open the box; there was a nice Asian outfit inside; neatly folded and a turban and a pair of decorative stone studded slippers, a small jewellery box; with a ring and a chain and gold buttons for the Asian outfit. But on top of all these was an A4 exercise book. Raza couldn't understand the motive for keeping these items separately; he opened the exercise book and saw, it is filled with an unknown script; Bengali; which he could neither read nor write. Nonetheless; he took everything out of the box and went to Dulal uncle's house.

That evening after dinner; he told Dulal uncle about the things he had found in the wooden box in the attic and his inability to read what has been written left for him by his father. Raza though hesitated to request help from Dulal uncle to decode what was left for him only; seeing the pain in his face, Dulal uncle asked him to bring the exercise book; knowing that the best chance Raza has; to know what is written there is through him.

The book was an apology letter from a broken man to a son; it started with his dreams of leaving Bangladesh despite his status at that time. His initial struggle; to pay the agent and ultimately arriving into France; fully unsuitably dressed to combat the temperature in Paris; at mid March. Outside the tube station; there was knee deep snow put aside by snow ploughs. His thin jumper; cotton blazer and sandals were inappropriate for that weather.

He shivered and jolted through the streets with his kit bag on the shoulders until he met Imran; in the cafe who took him to Samu Social, the social service that provided emergency accommodation to him and many others. Together; with Imran he crossed over to the UK on the back of a vegetable truck with twelve others that included two African women and two young children.

After leaving Dover; the driver opened the gates; allowing them to come out at a place near Essex and Shan and Imran took the train to London, the next week he found a job and moved to Helston.

The next testimony; was about his sexual molestation as a child; when tendering the goats on the flood plains; he was lured by a man; in his shackle who asked him to face the wall; giving a one paise sweet in his hand and when he was busy licking it; he rubbed his penis on his bare bumps, telling him that it will give him magical powers like the old man himself and he can have more sweets. He had to keep his promise; not telling anyone about it otherwise; he will never gain the magical powers. The man's shackle was washed away at night during the monsoon floods and his body was discovered downstream when Shan went to see it with other children from the relief camp.

When he first met Dulal at Manchester; for reasons unknown; they clicked quite quickly, may be because Dulal was in charge of the restaurant staff and soon Shan proved himself indispensible. He couldn't realize when that manager- employee relationship faded and the new relationship was forged that became the most prominent of all relationships he ever had.

The first day at the Gay Club was a nervous, scared and excited mixed feeling. Like a kid, he remained close to Dulal, wearing the best outfit and the hair done properly, as it was an important day. Dulal introduced him to other members of the group as his partner. He felt a kind of weird as though the club was full of people but Dulal only talked to few guys within his group; the rest were unknown. They remained in the outside bar area, there was loud music, men dancing on the platform and drinking and a seemingly unending stream of people entering the club. Shan was extremely uncomfortable in the new environment and was finding harder to breathe, as he could neither understand the music nor the conversation Dulal was having with others; he felt neglected. Sweat was dripping from the top of his head, down back, through the cracks all the way down to his toes. He wanted to leave immediately when he received a simple "hello." A guy who he had met at the restaurant worked as a waiter for few days came up to him. He could see that Shan was shaken and asked him to chill out.

Gradually as he started visiting the club on every Tuesdays; he felt more at home, became closer with a fun group of guys and most importantly, he started to feel like part of the community.

Working all day in the kitchen and with one day off had transformed him into a work machine; and everything he knew outside the restaurant was the club, he being used to it.

But the real challenge to the strength in the relationship was tested during the time of his detention by the Immigration authorities; Dulal was heartbroken and travelled to see him at the Detention Centre frequently. Though Dulal had confided to Ms Sen about the relationship but with little sympathy for 'third country homosexuals' in the UK, at that time she advised Shan to follow the other route.

When Shan came out of detention between them they had the most elaborate celebrations. The relationship has never stopped but in between; on and off; Shan had felt remorse for being different; outside the realm of his religious precept. Everything was fine; until he visited Bangladesh after many years. His feelings for Zoya were real and he believed that the marriage will change his life for good. But luck was not in his side; however; the news of Zoya had a child gave him the opportunity to tie the untied knot and he did all his best to mend it.

There was no lucky man than him when he successfully managed to pass on British nationality to Raza, the long waiting outside the Heathrow terminal for Raza and his mother was anxious and not fake.

The starting of a new life in the UK, with his wife and child didn't materialize; not because of him and him alone but the multiple reasons; his mother's affair, the mess-up with her case by the Immigration officials that landed them under the same roof with Dulal and the last nail in the coffin; the DNA test that failed to establish his paternity with Raza.

However; he always believed that the results were wrong and he is the real father; never even bothered to ask his mother; to clarify.

It was his sheer bad luck that everything ended so abruptly and he never had the chance to say goodbye to Raza. Though; he had not missed his mother so much but he missed Raza in everyday of his life particularly after the retirement; when he had ample time to introspect his life starting from the beginning.

Though he had tremendous respect for Dulal all his life but at some point; he envied him for the miracle that kept him protected from the most dreaded of the medical causes.

Towards the end; everyday getting up with the pain and the fear of being able to endure it the whole day and every day for the rest of his life was driving him mad. He wanted to escape from it; the discussion about death openly at the 'Death Café' gave him the moral boost and helped to uplift his spirit for a short time.

The last few pages were only the descriptions of the side effects of his medication and his deliberate skipping of some of the pills that made life more painful.

The writing ended there; with no date on any of the pages; it was impossible for Raza or Dulal to find out when he stopped writing and put it in the box.

However; in the last page of the exercise book; written up-side down was a personal letter for Raza; telling him that all the belongings were those wore by him on the day of his marriage and he must not destroy them but take back to England and he wrote; " I'm sorry. I'm so sorry for letting you down, for ignoring you and eventually leaving you because I didn't have the emotional strength to put everything aside and try to start a new life with your mother and you and I regret it now. We were a family and I failed to preserve it and I cannot change anything now. I'm sorry; I cannot change our past, but whatever I possess belongs to you and make sure that your future is bright as can be and never let your family down, and returned to your roots; if possible."

CHAPTER 43

Within the next two days; Raza had to clear the house to make way for viewings as the estate agents had a long list of potential buyers who were interested and Raza was in a rush. In the meantime; his solicitors gave the nod to sign the relevant paperwork; to become the legitimate owner of the house; the bank also released the money and the same transferred to his HSBC account in the UK.

Clothes, few crockery and all the furniture items went to the charity shop attached to the Death Cafe. Most of the kitchen items were picked up by the local Council on payment of a little money and taken for recycling.

The empty house looked much bigger and Raza bought a new mop-bucket, brush, hand gloves and cleaning solutions; to clean up the dirty floors that has been left untouched for almost six months and covered in thick dust.

It took him almost two days make it look squeaky clean; just before the first viewing commenced.

That afternoon; Raza managed to found a Monumental Mason, in the suburb of Helsinki and ordered a memory stone for his dad, getting the details from Dulal uncle over the phone, and reading; "It's so strange that when I finally understood him, and started loving the most; He has already left; called away by God, to his home; to rest. But; I am sure; that we will meet again someday;" Razaur Rahman.

The next two weeks was the waiting period; Raza didn't want to leave Helsinki without finishing his job; the day the headstone was to be erected Raza went back to the grave of his father; he bought flower seeds from the garden centre and spread over the grave; asking the caretaker to keep it tidy with the promise that he will be paid for his job.

As negotiations about the sale was going on; Raza returned to the sea-side every afternoon; where sitting alone; looking at the seagulls; he uncovered the layers of his father's life; his loves, friendships, dreams, disappointments, and the consequences of his choices. It is here that he discovered his father; to be an extremely confused man throughout his life; but despite his humble beginnings; he always harboured high ambitions and with his good luck that enable him to achieve whatever he deserved and he was born to work and losing his hand; didn't stop him. He also visited the Cafe; now owned by Akram; who gave his own version about his dad's caring nature and patience with a novice learner like him. Akram was still confident that it was only Shan's culinary skills that made the Cafe a success and it became a source of wealth for Dulal and him, but his journey ended pathetically and was not deserve of him; on the walls of the Cafe still hanging a commemorative photograph with the Chairman of the Local Commerce Council when they own the award at a Cooking competition.

Despite their strained relationship and he never looking up to him as the 'role model'; Raza understood; mistakes were from both sides; his parents could have an amicable solution in the matter that would have been beneficial for all parties. Instead; hounding two innocent men from their home, community, country and forcing forceful separation from everything was an act of cruelty and his mother was solely responsible for that; in that way she took her revenge with the person; who was so unblemished that; despite having a negative DNA report with his son; never questioned the fidelity of his wife but pretended to believe whatever was made to believe; to have peace and tranquility. He shouldn't be hallmarked as the most selfish; self centered and immoral person of all; as has been implanted by his mother. Even; after suffering so much; in his last days he truly missed his family. In conclusion; Raza genuinely believed that Dulal uncle had played an enormous role; influencing his dad in the decision making process; something he knew; he will never acknowledge.

When one of the viewers' gave an offer close to the asking price; Raza decided to agree with it. He was in a hurry; so everything was done in heist and to save the time; Raza agreed to pay the lawyers' fees, notaries' fees and registration fees; normally paid by the buyer.

Once the registration is completed; Raza left Finland but before leaving for good; he visited Shan's grave to pay his last tributes thanking him; for remembering him and promising him that he will pay back for his sins and will try his best to return to Bangladesh for good. He himself being unsure whether; his girlfriend; born and raised in East London will accept such a move.

CHAPTER 44

When Raza came back to London; he was a changed man; the IT employee at the High Street had already climbed to the riches by inheriting the money from overseas. But there was no apparent change in his life-style; except him deciding to buy a small two bedroom flat on the outskirts of London.

After much viewing; he decided to buy in Watford; a commutable distance from London. Though Yasmin was not happy with the purchase for unable to travel the distance every morning; to Leyton where she was a working as a teaching assistant. Raza insisted that she will easily find a similar job nearby. In regard to himself; he didn't mind travelling.

Raza wanted to spend each pence of the money he got from his late father sensibly; he never bought a car for personal use and relied on Public transport.

With his father being dead; there was no hesitation for Zoya to negotiate with Yasmin's family about the marriage; telling all kind of lies about Raza's father; except revealing his sexual identity.

Yasmin wanted a traditional marriage with the most fabulous and extravagant ceremony; after much research on the goggle; Zoya found the country house at Thornby Manor and was impressed when went to visit the venue with Yasmin and Raza.

They appointed a wedding planner and gave contract for halal catering to a renowned caterer.

The marriage was essentially divided into two parts; starting with the arrival of the groom and the traditional nikkah ceremony; conducted by the Muslim priest, followed by the lunch. In the afternoon the English registration ceremony, conducted by the Registrar.

The evening started with starters; photo session, followed by speeches; and the dinner. The sweet dishes were served separately. In the end was the closing ceremony; with entertainers and singers and traditional dancers to cheer up the guests.

On the wedding day; Yasmin looked absolutely gorgeous and stunning; draped in a dark red Indian wedding dress covered in sparkly jewels; complimented with flawless bridal makeup &

shimmering wedding jewellery. Raza also looked handsome in his Asian outfit; he wore the same turban; his father had worn on the day of his marriage.

They entered from the same door and sat at two corners; the Priest sat in the middle and after uttering the acceptance word was declared as husband and wife. After the priest has gone they sat in the middle holding hands and were blessed by family members and friends.

Soon lunch was announced; when guests left the bride and groom to have lunch at a separate hall. In that private moment Raza and Yasmin managed to have their first kiss after marriage; it was a beautiful moment and felt differently.

Soon Yasmin's friends came and the newly- wed couple joined the rest of the guests at the lunch hall. Whilst the manager announced that the Registrar has arrived and guests should get sifted to the Registration Hall.

As people hurried to the Registration Hall and took sits; Raza and Yasmin arrived together and stood on both sides of the table. After a brief introduction by the Registrar; Raza and Yasmin signed in the marriage registration book. Thereafter they pronounced the vows and exchanged wedding rings and were again declared man and wife by the Registrar. Cameras started clicking shots and the back door was opened to give way to an arched garden where the bride and groom stood and was photographed. The marriage was completed.

Yasmin and Raza retired to their private suit upstairs accompanied by few friends; they hardly had any rest; before friends started peeling off Yasmin's make-up to get ready for the evening reception.

Raza however had few hours of free time relaxing with friends when Yasmin's patience was put to test by the professional make-up artist.

It took more than two hours of arduous work by the make-up artist to make Yasim ready; and she still had some time to relax before the start of the evening ceremony at six o'clock.

At around; half-five the guests were served with starters and there were photo ceremonies in the lawn; until around half six guests were directed to the reception hall.

As the sun went down the scene looked amazing! When all décor elements shined brightly under the vivid lights, illuminating the whole ceremony creating a picture perfect moment; the stunning bride and groom entered the ceremony holding hands; Yasmin in an extravagant white wedding dress and Raza; a white Givenchy suit; they were accompanied by traditional female dancers and entertainers.

They went to the table and after sharing a toast; with all the guests sat down in the table and the speeches began. To save time; only Zoya; the bride's father and one of each of their best friends spoke. As soon as the bride and groom got seated the waiters became busy. There was constant rattling within the hall with a steady flow of multi course menu destined for the tables to satisfy the guests; who remain seated and enjoyed the food and non alcoholic drinks.

The speeches carefully drafted and precise; were read one after another; starting from Zoya and she didn't hesitate to take full credit for the upbringing of her son. In the end asking for blessings for her son and daughter-in-law; she ended it. Yasmin's dad managed to read from a piece of paper; written by Yasmin; he also requested everyone to shower their blessings for the newly wed. However; the speeches by Raza and Yasmin's closest friends' were interesting warning them about the other; in advance.

It took almost two hours to finish dinner; guests enjoyed the finest Bollywood songs; softly played as they enjoyed the sumptuous meal.

After; dinner guests were guided to the porch; where multiple sweet dishes of different colors and varying sweetness were served to the guests.

In the end; all the guests were guided to the reception hall and the party started; the couple have their first dance alongside a towering wedding cake and followed by carnival acts by friends and some professional performers who also boogied the night away with the wedding guests. The party ended at 1.00am in the morning and the guests were served with the wedding cake.

The bride and groom retired to the suite upstairs and all of the guests left; except Zoya as she dreaded to drive back to Manchester at 3.00am in the morning. She lay on the couch at the reception area and was waked up by Raza in the next morning.

The couple returned to their flat at Watford while Zoya travelled back to Manchester; she was so tired that almost slept on the wheels twice and was alerted by the rumbling sound of the white line; after being drifted towards the side barrier; forcing her to take frequent breaks.

Raza and Zoya set off for their short honeymoon; the next day; at a resort; in one of the islands; at the Seychelles archipelago where they had booked a suit; on a private island.

Flying from London Heathrow to Mahé was uneventful, from Mahé they took the ten minutes private boat ride to the island; they landed on their own private beach and straight way walked upto their suite; folding glass doors opening upto the sea. There was champagne & fruit in-room on arrival, gift vouchers to use at the Boutiques & for spa treatment, one for each.

In the next seven days; surrounded by one of the largest marine parks in the Indian Ocean, warm waters, private beach, spa, fine dining; Raza and Yasmin had the most wonderful time in the wonderland; as they did some diving; swimming and enjoyed the sun set and sun rise from their private beach; at the spa they were pampered from top to toe and the four excellent restaurants; where they had the experience of fine dining and served all kinds of food; from continental, Asian, Chinese to indigenous dishes.

They also signed up for yoga in the open pavilion in the balmy breeze and cycled together around the island. They also used the beach villa's pool at sunset. Raza and Yasmin remained within themselves between the two; but with so many things to do; they were really busy; before it was all over and it was time for them to return.

CHAPTER 45

Raza was commuting to Central London; but Yasmin gave up her job at the Hackney Borough and she registered herself with a Supply Teaching Assistant Agency; who started shifting her between schools locally. Though; initially sceptical; it was a higher pay; including the travelling expenses and no responsibility on her part and the move was so frequent; there were weeks when between 5 days; Yasmin worked at 15 different schools; in shifts. When other permanent staff's were grumbling about the workload; Yasmin hopped from one place to another; assisting children with special needs to help them follow the specially designed individual curriculum set for each child.

Despite the apparent stability; good job; flat in London, a functional social and community life within the city where he had spent more than two decades; Raza couldn't forget the letter left by his father; asking him to leave England for good. But whenever he tried to raise the issue with his mother and wife; he faced criticism and discourage.

His mother; have always insisted that Shan destroyed her life; and she couldn't accept the idea that her son; whom she had brought up alone; is now returning to Bangladesh; on advise of his deceased father; at the strength of his money. Raza had to plead with his mother to understand that he is not reliant on his money; he will be earning enough to have a good life in Bangladesh; particularly in Dhaka, one of the fastest growing metropolis' in the world and with the world getting smaller by day; he will be able to afford more luxuries there. Yasmin; can start a Private English medium school; in one of the booming townships that will have successful business from the start. With; no children it was the perfect time for them to make the move.

Zoya; had always her own way; she tried to influence Raza through her patience, kindness and consistency; trying to highlight the adversaries and risks involved with such a move; starting from crime, weather conditions; natural disasters, power shortage, corruption and poor medical facilities. She even tried to push him for counselling.

But Raza had been proud of his Bangladeshi origin; though he had inherited British citizenship by birth but that was a misguided proposition by his mother. Apart from being a

Bangladeshi; as a Sylheti; his parents being from Sylhet; Raza had always identified himself as a British Bengali, his background from Oldham and university student life and working life in London and living at the East London boroughs, with large concentration of Bangladeshis; he perfectly spoke and understand the language; in varied accents.

Raza started looking for jobs; in the IT sector; in the capital; Dhaka, posting his CV to various companies; patiently waiting for the suitable offer.

Initially rejecting a number of offers; he seriously took the offer by a multinational company; making in-roads into the blooming economy of Bangladesh. He applied for the post that was responsible for the IT infrastructure within the various cities of the country.

After; initial correspondence through emails; Raza was invited to attend an interview at Dubai; the investor being an Arab Sheikh.

When he was attending the interview at Dubai; Raza was already offered a job in Dubai which he immediately rejected; despite the grandeur buildings, malls, clean wide roads and the man made gardens and parks within the city; Raza didn't like the arid sands everywhere; his memory of Bangladesh with lush green fields; trees; water bodies and the huge river was irrevocable.

So when Raza was offered the job in Dhaka; he took up the opportunity; knowing very well that he and his family will have a wealthy life style; he would have a bigger house, a better car and staff to look after most of their needs; with plenty of cheap labour available where half the population was living on less than a dollar a day.

After 32 years in the UK, ultimately the day arrived when Londoner; Razaur Rehman left the UK with his wife to have one month induction period in Bangladesh; before deciding the final time whether to take up the challenge or continue with their lives in the UK.

Yasmin; had never been to Bangladesh; she was still holding her favorite Starbucks' Caramel Frappuccino when boarding the Qatar Airlines flight scheduled for Dhaka, and it was still cold, but the blended ice had already melted, it turned lighter brown with white foam on top. Sipping the icy-cold sweetness felt especially relaxing. She was wearing a thin white jacket and light blue jeans.

Though Yasmin was irked by the slight pushes and looks of Bangladeshi men returning home from the many Gulf countries and she was already missing London but travelling on the business class; paid by Raza's new employer meant; Yasmin's experience of travel in economy class for that particular stretch was saved for the future. But when using the toilets; she noticed men changed into lungis and sitting with both feet up on the seat; on the other side.

In the business class; there were few passengers; and most of the sits were empty; a skinny, tall business man who was wearing a black, custom-made summer suit was sitting behind Raza. There was a mother and her son; in one row and then there was an older European couple.

After almost an eight hour flight; the Pilot alerted the passengers; as the plane hovered over the capital city; Dhaka, Yasmin noticed an unplanned urban set-up covered in a haze of dust.

When Raza and Yasmin came out of the airport with their baggage's; they were already exhausted being heckled by the porters inside and their trolley snatched away following Raza's refusal to hire them; so they had to carry their luggage by hand.

With the mercury reaching 35degree Celsius and the orange sun overhead; it was whole new experience for Raza and Yasmin. Yasmin was already sweating profusely and by the time they were spotted by the emissary from Raza's company and shifted to the company car; a sparkling Toyota Avensis with leather seats; they both were exhausted and Yasmin's white coat and light blue jean's was covered with a thin film of black dust.

As the car pulled off through the busy streets of Dhaka; to take them to their new home; Yasmin had the first experience to have an actual look into the city; from where her parents belong and returning to her roots was an amazing feeling but within herself; she was not feeling that excited. All she wanted was everything for them to go terribly wrong; so that Raza decides to return to London after the induction period.

While Raza and the company emissary; Naz were busy conversing; trying to convince Raza about the economic stability of Bangladesh, as part of the G26, with a booming economy that did not so much as falter whilst the rest of the world weathered the brunt of the financial crisis and within it Dhaka; on the rise as a must-watch global city.

The driver was busy avoiding unruly traffic and the crowd most of whom were walking on the road avoiding the footpath and crossing the roads in between running cars. Yasmin was peeping outside; despite such crowd and obstruction; she was quite amused to feel the car moving at a high speed excessive of permissible limits within the UK localities.

Then she saw; the shackles besides the multi-storied shopping malls and high rises; that were quite a contrast. There were children running between the cars and hawking goods; many of them topless and without caring for their safety. Yasmin was shaken; as a little boy started banging on the car window on her side from outside; showing some artificial flowers when it stopped at a traffic signal and kept doing so even when the lights became green and the cars started moving.

As Yasim; almost lost her cool and asked the driver to stop; he calmly replied that; "If I stop for them at every signal; we will never reach home; Madam. I have more than 25 years experience in driving in the city and I am fully confident and capable of avoiding the hawker boys who are specially trained to target the expensive cars. Because they regularly bribe the traffic wardens; they are protected by the Police; and NGO's are unable to remove the boys from the streets for rehabilitation and integration to normal life."

Unfortunately, within the short journey; Yasmin could easily see that while many of the city's residents live in abject poverty, the other part doesn't always seem to visibly care, using humans as pawns; corruption is rife in the city and this was an intense shock to her.

CHAPTER 46

Raza was offered accommodation in the posh area; at Uttara; close to the Airport, a big bungalow surrounded by high walls and gated; manned by security staff 24 hours. Inside the house was centrally air conditioned; with marble floors; spiral staircase and huge rooms and breathtaking granite bathrooms and toilets. The furniture also suitably matched the house. There was a big garden on the back and on both sides. They were also provided with a cook, two maidservants and two servants.

Raza's office was in the up market district of Dhaka; and it took him more than an hour in the busy morning rush hour. Raza was in real shock to get used to at work; where everyone called their superiors by 'sir'; he had 200 people calling him; it every day.

He was surrounded by an entourage; every time; since he entered the office before 9.00 am till he left for home in the evening; most of the days; after 9.00pm. His staffs even asking to carry his bag; which Raza had to politely refuse; each time. Despite; repeatedly telling them, to call him by his name; his men were unable to grasp it.

However; as days passed by Raza clearly realised that Bangladesh is really comfortable, it's got all those good things, that he was unable to afford in London, but only if you can afford it. If you are struggling financially then it is like hell. However; one thing Raza realized that people here have little expectations and tries to be content within their means.

Also; in between the days; Raza had to travel to Chittogong and Khulna; to attend the inauguration ceremony of their local branches and he was the star attraction; holder of a red passport and spoke in a British accent. Travelling to the hilly terrain of Chittogong by the local Jet Airlines plane was a breathtaking experience; the plane wobbled and squabbled during landing and takeoff, a few hours day trip to Patenga and spending some time in the warm temperate waters of the Bay of Bengal was a pleasure experience. The Chittogong hill tracts reminded him of the Pennines; he having spent his entire childhood on the fringes of the dales.

While Raza was busy trying to set down his roots to the country; Yasmin had practically nothing to do but soon; she managed to make friends with some local ladies with the help of her common housemaid who informed her about the kitty parties arranged by the women on their block. Soon; Yasmin was invited to one such party; where everybody was very nice to her and welcomed her warmly. Soon; she managed to forge friendships with few women; through whom she had the real experience of life in Dhaka.

Yasmin learned to wear the sari; she started putting henna in her hands and bindis on her forehead, she even purchased glass bangles to match her clothing. Together; with the ladies group she had the real experience of life in Bangladesh; eat some of the local fish, visited the ghats on the Padma; she also enormously enjoyed, the National Mother Language Day on February 21, that aroused within her; the sense of self pride for being able to speak the language.

Because; the office car; went with Raza everyday and remained with him; Yasmin had no other alternative but to try out all the different modes of transportation; which she genuine believed is not for the faint-hearted, particularly the rickshaw, running between heavy vehicles on the main road.

Though they had a cook in the house; Yasmin hardly ate lunch at home; she tried all sorts of food at various restaurants and sometimes at roadside food joints; from burgers, kim chi, pad thai or pasta to fish curry and rice and the food always tasted better.

Yasmin; also found Dhaka; as a fantastic place to shop; because she had initially took limited clothing and it was apparently becoming certain that they will be in Dhaka for long; she actually had to shop for the sake of necessity. She also purchased traditional handloom saries from Old Dhaka for her mother and aunties, the amazing of all she quickly learned the art of bargaining reducing the actual price to almost fifty percent of the asking price.

Raza's high ranking position within the company came with many perks; including club memberships; situated in pockets within posh quarters of the city; with lush green golf courses, swimming pool, squash, tennis, badminton courts and bars, massage parlours and yoga centre; where a lot of foreigners can be found hanging around.

Yasmin often went and played badminton at the Gulshan Club; and enjoyed herself a drink of mango martini. She also liked the message at the Spa for a minimal price; as little as $4.

Often; on the Sunday afternoons; when their friends were busy with their extended families; Yasmin and Raza's personal favourite destination, was the Ramna Park; where acres of parkland and lake; gave them the sense of being close to the UK.

When visiting the many five star sparkling hotels; in Dhaka; to attend parties hosted by Raza's company; Yasmin had always wondered how in a country where millions of people suffer from the hardship of poverty; there could be such a display of disproportionate wealth. She had always liked her sojourns at the road-side stalls; best. Moreover; she never had the opportunity to attend parties at five star hotels in London even once, in fact none of her family members had even visited them.

Initially; Raza's induction period was fixed for a month but with the company expanding at tremendous speed; as one top boss', the return ticket for London; had to be postponed simultaneously and eventually had to be cancelled.

Yasmin was on her yearly leave and after it had expired with no sign of return to London; she emailed her resignation letter to the agency office; she was enrolled with, requesting them to forward a reference letter by email.

Unknown of the extended stay; Yasmin had also left her qualification certificates in London; at Watford which her sister failed to gather from the mess. So she requested the agency with copies of her certificates to forward the same.

Soon Yasmin was getting bored with her monotonous life; she wanted to get rid of her high class friends; in the neighbourhood; she being fed-up to continue with the competition to display; who has the most.

She found out from her maid-servant; Runa that the missionaries had opened a charity school recently, in their slum where slum children are provided free meals and free education. A tall man; wearing a long rob and big silver cross; also visits the school every Thursdays and gives sweets to the children and plays with them. He can't speak "Bengali".

The next Thursday; Yasmin made-up her mind to visit the school; in her maid-servant's slum, she being determined to do something worthy, when Yasmin reached the tin shade build on the new land adjacent to the cremation ghat of the Hindus; the stink of flesh immediately stuck her. Inside the classroom; there was a group of children of different age groups hurdling together and a pale young girl standing in front of the blackboard. In the corner facing towards the wall was a tall figure; busy on his small work desk; he remained undisturbed by the commotion as Yasmin intruding the learning session and forced the teacher to stop. Already informed by Runa; Yasmin walked past the students and went straight to the man; as she called from the back to introduce herself; Father; Joseph Perriera; turned back and immediately stood up from his sit. Unwilling to disturb the class comprising of children; some of whom will rush to work; immediately after school, Father Perriera walked outside the classroom with Yasmin and they walked into the next shade which is used as a kitchen. Hearing Yasmin's accent; Father Perriera was taken by surprise; that she is willing to get involved with the school; situated in such an impoverished locality when any renowned missionary school in Dhaka will recruit her with a high salary.

However; seeing Yasmin's enthusiasm; Father Perriera couldn't disqualify her but warned her that there's a bunch of swindlers and freaks out there in the slum, and they seem to love either harassing women, or foreigners, or both and with her accent; Yasmin could be easily classified as one. Therefore; he proposed that he will arrange for a local social worker to accompany her outside the slum after school.

Raza's reaction to her selection of work; as "a social worker" though not entirely negative; but he warned her; not to be there after dark and not to show too much skin; given the pervasive nature of the conservatism in such societies and to remain vigilant at all times for she being involved with charity through the Missionaries that can irk locals at any time.

Within two months into the school; Yasmin's students started speaking English; they had no choice but to learn the language as their "madam" could only speak English and her Bengali was pathetic.

Yasmin was particularly teaching the elder children; many of the boys were hawkers and the girls helped their mothers; employed as housemaids. Because; most of the children had no further time to study except at school; Yasmin pushed them hard. She was teaching Maths and English while the other teacher; was covering the other subjects. Because; Yasmin had realised that only teaching them the subjects without any qualifications will be of little help for them in future. She forced Raza to secure some funds through her company and Father Perriera; managed to send three qualified teachers from; St Gregory's High School to help the children with other subjects.

Amongst the six children; aged 12- 14 years; they were picking up fast and it was a challenge for Yasmin; to make them successful in the Year 10 examination; in two to three years time. Her involvement with the school; in fact changed her life so much that she hardly had time for anything. She also stopped missing London; her family, friends and everything she was used to and her challenging task meant; it was impossible for her to leave.

Yasim had no holidays and she even started coaching the children at home on Sundays; to prepare them and spoke excitedly whenever the children showed progress. In the meantime; as Raza's company was pressing him to take up the post on a permanent basis; therefore the couple had to make plans to visit London and wrap up everything before returning to Bangladesh for good.

CHAPTER 47

Yasmin and Raza returned to the UK after a long eight months with the plan to sell the flat in London; clear it up, spent at least one week in Oldham and return back to Bangladesh.

Though Yasmin had left a key with her brother and phoned him before to clean up; it was in total mess. Also; finding that they have returned to Watford; the phone never stopped for the first few days and everyone wanted to meet them to share their understanding of life in a third world country; like Bangladesh.

Almost every night they had invitations from friends and family members; everyone seemed to be very enthusiastic to learn about their experiences; such inquisitiveness from friends and family members lead to a feeling in Raza and Yasmin that they are being special. But soon; they managed to pick up the narrow mindedness of many of them through their taunts about the social structure, religious conservatism, transport, pollution, the daily prayer calls and the list was exhaustive. But Raza and Yasmin's polite response that they had fallen in love with the city; even made the awful critic quiet.

Raza and Zoya donated all the staff they had within the first two weeks and instructed the local Selling Agent to set up a viewing day for all potential buyers in one day; from morning till evening; with an asking price of £200,000.

On a Saturday; from morning 9.00am there was a queue in front of the building as people lined up for viewing; there were more than 100 viewers on that single day and at least four people offered the same price; forcing the agent to give it to the highest bidder amongst them. Raza's flat was sold for £215,000.

After signing the sale contract; Raza and Yasmin decided to spend the last week of their stay in the UK, with Zoya, in Oldham it was Yasmin's first visit to her mother-in-law's house and it was Raza's bond with his mother that inspired his decision.

Raza; knew that his decision had made her hurt and angry as she wanted to erase Bangladesh from her mind; all these years and it was not her fault. She had been a victim always and her fight to keep herself going; despite everything that happened to her; deserves respect and admiration. Raza had enormous respects for his mother; if it was not her; he wouldn't have probably finished high school.

But during his last visit; Raza found her mother with many 'negative emotions', one moment she was very happy to see Raza and Yasmin happy together; other moment she was not. She was visibly struggling with a diversity of thoughts; and was unable to perform all personal and social roles efficiently, at home. When during a conversion after dinner; Zoya directly told Raza and Yasmin that how she feels at times about the world is not a beautiful flowery place and struggles to fight these 'negative' emotions; Raza couldn't believe himself. He wanted her to seek medical help which she denied telling that she should have the right to have control over the feelings; she experiences without being a guinea pig.

Zoya though blatantly refused to go to Bangladesh at any time but Raza knew that she will definitely not hesitate to visit him during the school holidays upon his request.

Seeing his mother struggling, Raza felt guilty; thinking that he shouldn't have left her and settled in London, in first instance.

Raza adored his mother and it was this particular quality; the respect for his mother that impressed Yasmin, initially. But his ability to stand up to his mother and not letting her control him, not fearing his mother and not putting his mommy first; also demanded respect.

But because of his particular childhood and adolescent, Raza had realized very early in his life that he was all his mother had but despite that she never wanted him to compensate for her loses. Their relationship had been always healthy not requiring Raza to put her above everything; she had never being demanding and a huge hug from him was all she desired.

Raza never feared about his mother getting angry with him or not speak to him if he disappoints her and didn't do everything she asked. Instead; he knew that his mother's love is unconditional and often disappointed her knowing that his mother will eventually get over it.

Raza had always cherished the time, he spent with his mother particularly since in his late teens they laughed together, reminisce their past and had heartfelt talks. So seeing her negative feelings was indeed worrying for Raza.

He could never deny that it was her warmth and closeness that was critical to shape his life as a teenager and it has matured with time. Raza; can never cause harm to anybody knowingly and is always considered to be friendly, considerate and accommodative. Everyone; close to him knows that he doesn't know; to complain. Though; he had some temperament during the adolescence days but he soon grew over them during his late teens; particularly after leaving home; to study at London.

When Raza left home; aged 18 years to Study Computer Science at the East London University; he lacked many good skills; but luckily his housemate who was two years older and had lived out of home for about 5 years by that stage, was quite open and polite with advice and criticism. It was while living separately; Raza learned to understand that people come from lots of different household environments and they all have different ways of doing things — and everyone thinks their way of doing something is the right way and the only way!

But his qualities; understanding of the people, resilience, respect for others and caring nature; helped him to learn quicker than others and Raza always believed that these are the qualities; he got from his mother.

Another thing he learnt to take care; the same time was the cost of living; when living with his mother; he had no worries but it soon became a difficult task to balance everything with the subsistence money he was getting at that time; paying for the bills, rent, groceries, phone bills, insurance etc. and soon found that he was no longer in a situation where he was able to go to the movies, out to meals and shopping with friends constantly due to limited finances, and it was a bit depressing but he learned to plan some at home activities with friends to avoid feeling isolated and embarrassed. The financial struggle in his student life indeed made him not being a squanderer in later life.

Fortunately; Raza had never experienced homesickness; even though he was very close to his mother. So even after finishing university; he never thought of returning to the northwest. Though he didn't hesitate to seek his mums guidance for situations; he was unable to deal with but living alone; enabled him to learn and adjust to various situations. But one thing has been sure always to communicate with his mum regularly and thanking her for all she ever did for him.

Although; Raza's cooking skills improved a lot while living alone but since marriage; he started relying on his wife who was in all means a better cook.

Raza was worried for his mother; but he knew; she was a real fighter and will manage to defend herself whatever may come. As a primary school teacher; with little children around and their weird thoughts and expressions brought the healing touch to her mind; with them she had no inhibitions and need not to measure her expressions; she was 100% happy.

CHAPTER 48

While in Oldham; Raza took Yasmin everywhere; even to see the house on the Pennine Hills where he had lived initially and went to his first school. The streets of Oldham seemed stood still over the years with little or no change at all. Dulal uncle's house was however demolished to give way for a new Old Age Home. He even took Yasmin to see the Hadrian's Wall and went for dinner at Jalnupur Restaurant; renamed Desi Dhaba and owned by a Punjabi.

The walk in the woods alongside the stream behind their back garden was very exciting for Yasmin; who never thought that such greenland could be present behind someone's backyard.

Understanding; her sentiments and feeling of sadness due to separation; Raza bought his mother an iphone and a laptop; installing them both; so that she can have video conferencing with him and Yasmin whenever she choose. He also offered to pay the rest of the mortgage for the house; to make her worry less which she instantly denied; telling it acts as the motivation; to get up every morning and rush to school.

Seven days was a very short time and it passed without alarm; and eventually the day arrived to leave Oldham and England for good.

Raza didn't want his mum to drop him and Yasmin at Manchester Airport but had to agree in the end following insistence from her. The flight was at half twelve in the afternoon; so they had to leave home; after breakfast. During the entire journey; Zoya constantly gave advice to Raza and Yasmin about the dos and don'ts in Bangladesh, she seemed particularly worried for Yasmin; knowing that she works in the slum. Raza and Yasmin's repeated assurance that Dhaka is not Sylhet and things have changed in Bangladesh more recently failed to assure her.

On reaching the Airport after booking the luggage; Zoya opened her handbag and gave parting gifts to the couple; two wrists watches; specially made with her initials embalmed in them and card; telling them to open it later. Hugging her; both Raza and Yasmin moved in for security checks and Zoya kept waving; when she turned back; her eyes were wet. She still felt the warmth of her son; the very day they arrived at London.

As the plane was towed towards the runway; suddenly Raza started missing his mother wandering whether she had already reached home; soon the plane was in acceleration and was out in the air.

From the window; Raza kept looking down; there is all sorts of human activity: the tiny cars were still visible and rows of houses; football pitches; soon he could only see big square green patches; trying to speculate what grows in those lands. The sky was unusually clear; and everything below was almost clearly visible; the glance of England from the sky; which Raza had paid no attention at any time before; but this time he could distinctly feel the pain of separation from the land; and everything else; he was leaving behind. Within himself; he was literally struggling to reason with his decision to part from everything and anything; he always thought belonged close to his heart; trying to make himself understand that in reality; he got everything by fluke; not obtaining legitimately; but leaving behind his mum alone; brought a sense of guilt. Suddenly with a jolt the plane moved up and after a moment's indulgence when Raza looked down; England had disappeared beneath the dense white clouds which looked like fresh snow and the plane moving over it.

Raza's rendezvous with oneself was disturbed by Yasim who had reached out to the card given by her mother-in-law and was trying to draw his attention; when he looked at her; she read the card; with a fumbling voice; "I'll leave the future up to you. It's unwritten; I don't know if; it will last more than I have anticipated. But I certainly know that the world doesn't end within the four walls. I hope you'll grow into it, learn to live in it, no matter how hard it is out there. Because you're a part of me, and you know; how I have done in here, I'll always be a part of you even when I'm not here."